PHOENIX

Asphalt Cowboys

2

MADISON SEVIER

Copyright © 2016 by Madison Sevier

2 MADISON SEVIER

ALL RIGHTS RESERVED: This literary work may not be reproduced or transmitted in any form or by any means, including electronic or photographic reproduction, in whole or in part, without express written permission of the author, **Madison Sevier**.

All characters and events in this book are fictitious. Any resemblance to actual persons living or dead is purely coincidental.

This eBook is licensed for your personal enjoyment only. This eBook may not be re-sold, reproduced in any format (digital, paper, audio or video format) or given away to other people without the written permission from the author. If you would like to share this eBook with another person, please purchase an additional copy for each recipient. If you're reading this book and did not purchase it, or it was not purchased for your enjoyment only, then please return to your favorite retailer and purchase your own copy. Thank you for respecting the hard work of this author.

WARNING: The unauthorized reproduction in any format or distribution of this copyrighted work is illegal. Criminal copyright infringement, including infringement without monetary gain, is investigated by the **FBI** and is punishable by up to **5 years** in federal prison and a fine of **$250,000**.

4 MADISON SEVIER

PHOENIX, Asphalt Cowboys 2

Copyright © 2016Madison Sevier

ISBN: 1537028502

ISBN 13: 978-1537028507

Cover Created by SMB Designs

Copyright © 2016Madison Sevier

6 MADISON SEVIER

TABLE OF CONTENTS

DEDICATION

CHAPTER ONE

CHAPTER TWO

CHAPTER THREE

CHAPTER FOUR

CHAPTER FIVE

CHAPTER SIX

CHAPTER SEVEN

CHAPTER EIGHT

CHAPTER NINE

CHAPTER TEN

CHAPTER ELEVEN

CHAPTER TWELVE

CHAPTER THIRTEEN

CHAPTER FOURTEEN

CHAPTER FIFTEEN

CHAPTER SIXTEEN

CHAPTER SEVENTEEN

CHAPTER EIGHTEEN

CHAPTER NINETEEN

CHAPTER TWENTY

CHAPTER TWENTY-ONE

CHAPTER TWENTY-TWO

CHAPTER TWENTY-THREE

EPILOGUE

DEDICATION

For everyone who has ever wanted to spread their wings and fly. Don't wait. Life's so very short.

Many, many thanks to my husband, Mike. Thank you for the reference material, knowledge, infinite support and love you've given to me. You mean the world to me. My one and only.

P.s. The name you chose for Savannah and Mason's baby is absolutely perfect. It will live on in this story forever as will my love for you.

10 MADISON SEVIER

PROLOGUE

Twenty years ago, Virginia

"I'm really sorry, Ms. Chapin. I wish we could've made this work. He's just..." the woman lowered her voice to a whisper, attempting to prevent the ten-year-old boy from overhearing, "damaged. I don't think you truly understand what type of child we were hoping for, but it isn't him."

If being the son of two cokeheads who sold anything—including their bodies, to anyone who was willing to get them high—and often right in from of him, was a reason to be 'damaged', then, yeah he probably was. Up until they'd been arrested for child abuse, child neglect and slapped with drug paraphernalia, drug possession and solicitation charges, he'd had to watch it occur repeatedly on a daily and nightly basis. When they'd finally been thrown in jail, he'd seen them at their absolute worst for as long as he could remember. No child should have to watch his or her own parents drugged out of their minds and prostituting themselves for the first eight years of his or her life. Luckily, they'd signed away their rights to their only son as soon as they were given the opportunity.

He watched as Ms. Chapin gently placed her hand on the woman's arm and led her from the office, looking at him with eyes full of sadness; just like she'd done every other time his forever home didn't quite last that long. His most recent escapade into the world of pretending as if he had a real family had lasted eleven days—a new record for him. He liked this last family enough, but they were right. He wasn't what they needed or wanted.

It wasn't as if he tried to get them to return him to the orphanage. He hated coming back. Nevertheless, there was something about him that no one liked—certainly not enough to accept him as he was and help him to become what he was meant to be. He never acted out or behaved in any way that could've been deemed disrespectful. Each day, he went to school and came straight home to do his chores and homework. His goal was to be the perfect little boy they'd wanted. All of them. He'd become so accustom to adapting his behavior for each family that had taken him into their home, he didn't remember much about who he truly was anymore and to be honest, forgetting his past would be fine with him.

One family wanted the sporty kid—he couldn't catch a ball if his life depended on it. Another wanted him to join the church choir and he truly tried, but couldn't hold a note. Besides, he didn't believe any god would allow a child to live through what he'd lived through. God was supposed to love children not let them be born to degenerates such as his parents were. The long lists of why he didn't fit in anywhere changed with each pair of potential parents. The one fact remained—he wasn't their kid and he'd never be their perfect child. No matter where he went, things changed soon after he'd get all settled in and he'd adapt to what he thought they wanted from him in the hopes that he'd finally be good enough. Each rejection was different and more painful in its own way.

The only thing that had remained the same was his silence. He didn't say much at all for fear he'd say the wrong thing with the wrong tone or at the wrong time.

His birth parents and two of the prospective families he'd lived with had seen to it that he knew just how much they hated anything he said and how he said it. He soon learned that his best bet was to stay quiet. One would think that his eager-to-please behavior would be something parents would want. A quiet kid? After all of the loudmouths he'd seen during his years at the children's home, why wouldn't a well-behaved kid be a blessing?

Bottom line, he'd messed up again. Somehow.

"Are you all right?" Ms. Chapin had walked back into the room so quietly; he flinched when she spoke to him. She placed her hands, soft and familiar over his own. "I'm so very sorry it didn't work out with them. But don't worry, okay? We will find you the perfect family. You'll see. One day, they'll walk right through that door, see you and each of you will know it's right. You belong with people who can see how truly special you are and who can see what a strong young man you are. They're out there. I just know it."

He knew better but didn't want to ruin Ms. Chapin's attempt at making him feel better. "Sure. I know. May I go to my room now? I've got some homework to finish."

"Yes you may. See you at dinner. Tomorrow we'll work on a new plan to find you a forever home."

"Yes, ma'am." None of it mattered to him. When he grew up, he'd be a cowboy just like the ones on the television they were allowed to watch for an hour each day. He'd answer to no one and travel the country doing whatever he wanted, whenever he wanted.

Pulling the heavy oak door shut behind him, he felt numb inside as he headed back to the only stability he'd ever known. That very same oak door that he would close over and over again, as he was returned like a defective product while other kids were chosen. Younger, smarter, louder, skinnier, those with less of a *past* who were better prospects for having an honorable future were all welcomed into families who traveled from other states to find their perfect child or project, as he liked to think of them.

Sometimes people just needed to fix something that was broken. He'd met quite a few of those *fixers* and none had been made of the right stuff. They'd all been weak, looking for an easy DIY and he was far from that.

In fact, he'd soon decided to make a game out of it. Beating his old records and making new ones. On one occasion, he'd been returned in less than five hours. A personal best in his eyes. Before long, he made silent bets with himself on how long he'd get to stay with each of them and every time he was right.

The door seemed less intimidating and easier to close as he grew up. He'd lost count of how many times he'd been through it. Each time, it felt like a normal part of his everyday life. Until that final time on his eighteenth birthday when he was free to open the door and leave the orphanage on his own. After that day, the only thing he'd kept closed was his heart. Too bad his heart wasn't enough to protect him from the many more years of mistakes and failures he'd go through in the future. Apparently, he was born to be a loser.

CHAPTER ONE

Present Day, Northern Kentucky

Memories. Flashes from another time, another life. That's all.

He'd made it through everything life had thrown at him so far. He'd been strong enough to keep going. A multiple-time survivor. So why wasn't he strong enough to forget?

Maybe because you'll never be good enough or amount to anything more than that kid they tossed away like the trash you still are and will always be.

That incessant, fucked up voice always showed up when he had other things to do and worry about. Like the fact that the steel industry was stagnant and freight had been very, very slow for the past few months and he was crazy nervous about the fact he could lose everything all over again.

Stop being such a whiner. You'll bounce back. That is, if you stop thinkin' like a pussy.

"Aiden? You okay, man?" Jake 'Tex' Seymour sat across from him, tilting his head with a squint in his eyes.

"I'm fine. Why?" He leaned back in the cracked vinyl booth, reaching out for his cup of coffee that had now gone cold.

"Well, you sorta' spaced on us for a minute." Mason chimed in.

"I said I'm fine. What were you saying about damaged goods?"

Mason cleared his throat and Aiden raised his cup above his head, signaling the waitress that he was in need of more. "Just that their newest crane operator of the week fucked up the bands on three of my coils when he lifted them off the wagon. Now, their company has filed a loss for damaged products delivered by me—the driver. Assholes."

"Clearly they don't want to take responsibility for anything. Which shouldn't come as a surprise, but still." Jake chuckled, shaking his head.

Jake always had something to say about everyone else and he didn't care who heard it or whether they liked it or not. It was an admirable and annoying quality that most of the Asphalt Cowboys had. They were livin' life between the lines a hundred or more hours a week. At some point, they all stopped givin' a fuck about being polite or politically correct.

"Kind of like Romeo, right Mason?"

The look on Mason's face and the anger that flared in his eyes made it perfectly clear that Aiden's brain-to-mouth filter should've been used right then. Romeo was a raw subject for Mason. However, Aiden was tired of the handholding and bullshit behavior the dude got away with.

"You'd know all about that, wouldn't you?" Mason pinned him with a look.

"Really? What the hell, man? I was just kiddin' around. Relax."

Aiden watched as Jake covered his mouth with one hand, his eyes popped open, big and wide as he shook his head at him from across the booth as if to say "Bad move, man". Romeo was the one subject Tex would never bring up…not to Mason, anyways. Moreover, he'd said so many, many times.

"Look, the point of this conversation is that steel freight is movin' too slow and the clients we haul for are lookin' for reasons to take even more money away from us. But, I've got ideas on how we can fix it. Raisin' Kaine Trucking and its drivers are not goin' down with a sinkin' ship."

Aiden had been leased onto Mason's company and runnin' loads under his own authority for the past five years. If Mason couldn't grab them a coil, they all had other options—brokers or agents other than their friend Hayley Shaw to go through. He cared for her more than any other woman he'd ever met and it made collecting payoffs a bit more difficult than when they'd all run for her, but at least they weren't sittin' around with their thumbs up their asses. Loads were loads. Money was money. All Aiden cared about was rollin' on.

"So, what's the plan?" Jake seemed relieved to see the conversation headed in another direction.

"There's always produce from Texas or state fair rides. Each of us are equipped for just about anything. They won't starve us out. As long as y'all want to, our crew will clean house in any lane. No *hired* trucks can run the way we do. You know it and I know it."

"So ya want us to pull some renegade cowboy shit?" Aiden didn't really care that they'd be drivin' illegal hours because the money would be great. But, part of him—the newly responsible part, really dreaded the more-than-likely chance of getting' busted for something by the D.O.T.

According to the owner of the main company that Raisin' Kaine was leased to, Marcus Schenk, Mason's guys were famous for going rogue. No logs. No documented hours. No fucks to give. Marcus would wag his finger at them and verbally forbid their way of doing things, and all while winking at them. He's always been a "what I don't know won't hurt me, my company or my bottom line" kind of guy. Mason's guys lucked out when it came to Marcus Schenk. He'd covered their asses more than once and he always would as long as it also put money in his pockets. Raisin' Kaine Trucking had landed them too many accounts in the past to ever be considered a liability. Marcus Schenk knew whose palms needed to be greased and when. With the economy the way it was, Schenk would be toast if it weren't for Mason's drivers and their mash-that-gas-tote-that-ass way of getting things done.

"Why not? I'll know more in the next day or so. The latest word from Hayley Shaw is that we have three more companies goin' on shutdown to take inventory. I call bullshit on that one. It's just like it was in '08. We're about to watch shit hit the fan again." Mason raked a hand through his hair and tipped his neck side-to-side; a reflexive action Mason only did when he was worried about something. That cluster of movements meant all of them should also be worried.

Aiden had heard all of the stories of '08 and then the crapfest of freight for a few years after. Combine that with the huge jump in the cost of diesel as the economy took a dump and countless truckers hung it up, retired or went out to find factory jobs. Mason managed to make it through and he came back strong enough to build his company up to four trucks and a backup rig he kept in the barn in the event that any of theirs went down for any reason. Between the four of them, Aiden couldn't see any reason that they wouldn't make it through this next slump. Hell, he'd made it through worse without a damn penny to his name.

"Is Romeo on board?"

"Damn, man. Really? Why'd you bring him up again? Mason's gonna kick your ass." Jake wasn't foolin' anyone. He enjoyed seein' Mason get riled up. Hell, Jake had instigated plenty of Mason's rants. He was an easy mark.

"Seriously. If we're gonna do this, we should all be doin' it to save the company."

"No idea." Mason leaned forward; crossing his arms in front of him on the tabletop that looked like it'd been dragged through every hippie party in the 70s. The damn thing needed to be incinerated to destroy the number of germs that had most likely taken up habitat on and under it. Again, why had they stopped at that shitty hole in the wall? The place was a lot lizard's paradise. "Haven't spoken to him much lately. Been kinda hard to pin him down."

There was a sharpness to his clipped comments and stilted tone that Aiden should've seen as a warning, but he continued. "Still on a bender?"

"Yep. Had a decent sized payout five days ago. He went off to do his usual damage. He'll never learn."

"Man, he will. But it's gotta' be on his own terms. Trust me. I know better than all of you combined. Just stop savin' him. Stop loadin' him. Stop payin' him. He will learn." Aiden enunciated each of his last three words slowly.

"Oh, really? Ya know damn well where he's been. Didn't ya say you saw him three days ago when you were passin' through Indiana into Kentucky. You coulda' stopped him, Aiden. You shoulda' stopped him."

Mason's tone was one that Aiden had heard many, many times throughout his own life. One of disappointment combined with worry and anger. He took a deep breath, counting to twenty and weighing his own words before responding to Mason's heavily loaded comments.

"Man, the kid's not my responsibility."

Jake looked like he was pissin' himself and lookin' for a way to get outta' the booth and restaurant before all hell broke loose. But he was just as stuck as Aiden was.

"You." Mason pointed at him, reminding him of the many disappointed people he'd met in his life. "Of all people, you know what he's gotten himself into."

"Yes, I do and I got myself out of it. I also know the only way he'll get out of it is if he's either broke or finally sees the light on his own. Gambling is his drug. Eventually he'll want away from it." Or die trying. Aiden knew hard deep Romeo was into it. He'd been there himself. Only much, much worse.

"He's been outta money often and it didn't help. Now, I'm the one who's gonna' go broke bailin' his ass out again."

"Then stop fuckin' loadin' the kid. Starve him and hire someone else to pick up his damn slack. If there's no money, he can't gamble it away, spend it on booze or flaunt it to every hot piece of ass that shakes her ass in front of him. You're his big brother. Put your fuckin' foot down and deal with this shit. Enough is damn enough. Ya been savin' his ass all his life. He's a grown man, Mason. Stop fuckin' coddlin' him."

Aside from the anger flaring in Mason's eyes and the look of utter shock in Tex's, Aiden wasn't about to back down. He hadn't been the only one thinkin' Mason needed to step up and it was high time someone gave him what-for. If the rest of 'em were gonna' stay in the shadows, he was happy to be the one to nut-up and take him Mason to task. What could he possibly do to Aiden? Not load him? Big fuckin' deal. There was plenty of other freight to be had and plenty of money to be made elsewhere if it came down to that.

"That spoiled son-of-a-bitch needs his ass kicked and you know it, man. You gonna' do it or has becoming a husband with a baby on the way made you soft?"

Truth be told, Aiden hated having to speak those words to his longtime friend. But that's what friends were for. If your buddies couldn't tell it to ya' straight, what was the point? If someone long ago had cared enough about Aiden to kick his ass, maybe he wouldn't have fucked up so many times or had such a rough road to travel. He'd been knocked down by life, by his own hands dealing him a shitstorm of problems and for most of his past thirty years it'd felt like the shitfest of bad luck would never end. Countless years of highs and lows had plagued him, but he always found a way to climb out of whatever hole he'd found himself in. Sebastian, 'Romeo', didn't have that same resolve and they all knew it. Sure, Aiden knew all about the Kaine brothers' rough childhood. Who truly had an easy ride? Only Mason and Sebastian were responsible for what his life was now.

And by God, Mason needed a reality check as badly as his kid brother did.

"Seriously, Phoenix? Maybe *your* ass is the one that needs kicked?" Mason slid out of the booth, towering over them with his six-foot-plus build and fists clenched at his sides.

"Guys, guys. Calm the fuck down. Mason sit and for once in your life, fucking listen to your friends." Jake's words fell on deaf ears. To Aiden, Jake seemed to be bracing for shit to hit the fan.

"You'd really kick my ass for speakin' the truth, Mason? Bring it."

"Ya' really don't wanna' keep talkin', Phoenix."

"What are ya' gonna' do? Not load me? How 'bout we deliver these coils and you spend the next week gettin' your brother on track. With shutdown happening, seems like a good time to bust his ass. You deal with your shit and I'll see y'all when you're done."

Aiden tossed money for his bill onto the table and stood. Nose-to-nose with his friend, "I won't fight you. If you're lookin' for that kind of action, ya' need to take your immature ass elsewhere. I don't need this shit. And if ya' wanna' take it any further, I'll work elsewhere. You're not the only gig around."

Mason puffed out his chest, "Well, it's the only one who'd take your broke, gamblin' ass years ago. You'd best remember that, Phoenix. I did a lot for you when no one else would."

Now, Aiden didn't appreciate having kind gestures thrown back in his face and he wasn't one to stand for it. For everything Mason had done for him, he'd been repaid ten-fold within the past few months.

With a final pointed look, Aiden turned to leave. Stopping at the dilapidated door of the dirtiest shithole dive he'd ever set foot in, he tossed parting words over his shoulder before shoving the door open. "And you'd better remember what my *broke, gamblin' ass* did to make sure your pretty wife never had to set eyes on that bastard Vinny again." Aiden lowered his voice, "That *accidental overdose* might not have happened if I didn't have friends in low places and he'd have been out of prison someday. I'd say we're pretty fuckin' even, friend."

Man, what Aiden really needed was time off to see and talk to his best friend. The same friend who'd never see him the way he saw her. The woman he knew he was destined to be with. Sadly, she had one damn rule and he also knew she'd never break it…especially for a loser like him who lived life between the lines and had nothing substantial to offer her other than his heart. For a woman like Hayley, that'd never be enough.

CHAPTER TWO

"Savannah, I don't know how you do it. A baby on the way, Mason on the road and all of these beautiful creatures to care for by yourself. My office was so crazy, I had to hire help." Hayley Shaw cuddled the newest resident of Savannah's animal shelter, an adorable Chihuahua with a cream-colored coat, ears too large for his tiny face and a long beige stripe down the middle of his back. Holding him was the closest thing to Heaven she'd ever felt. The little guy was perfect—for whomever would adopt him eventually.

"Honestly, I don't know how I do it sometimes either." Smiling, she disappeared into the back room for a moment and returned with a plush, blue doggie bed. "This one should work. Hopefully, he'll approve. He's been here less than thirty-six hours and he's turned his nose up at just about everything I've given him."

"Maybe he's just depressed. I mean, what kind of piece of shit just drops off a ten-month-old puppy because it isn't the right color?" Hayley would never understand the cruel shit people did to animals. Luckily, there were people like Savannah to make up for the assholes in the world.

"You're right. About all of that. I've seen surrenders for the dumbest reasons. This little dude is potty-trained, he's quiet and hasn't caused one bit of trouble. And just look at those green eyes! He melts my heart each time I look at him." Savannah rubbed the little dog's chin and he stretched his neck out, thoroughly enjoying the attention.

When she met Savannah, it'd been the night before her wedding. Mason and she were a picture-perfect couple. Savannah, with her breathtaking gorgeous and curvaceous self, combined with Mason's rough and ruggedly handsome sexiness. Together, they were almost painful to look at. She could hardly believe someone like Savannah was with a trucker. Hayley had been around truckers for many, many years and she'd never ever consider dating one. Not because of anything they'd done. No, it was a personal choice based on her own past. However, those two made it look easy and lately, she'd thought about reconsidering her number one rule—never date a trucker. If she were to break that rule, she knew exactly who she'd want.

"So, what are ya' gonna' do on your week off, Hales? If you're up to it, I could use a hand around here. Ronnie won't be arriving until next week and Mason will be spending each day doing maintenance on the trucks while they're idle."

"Well, I've still got a lot of work to do even though there most likely won't be any loads out of the steel mills. But, I could stop by now and then if you really need me to. And I'd be happy to cuddle this little fella. Besides JoLynn will be able to hold down the fort. She's been a lifesaver with everything that's been happening." The tiny dog pressed himself against Hayley's chest and looked up at her with adoring eyes.

"He likes you. Who's JoLynn? Is she your new dispatcher?"

If she didn't find a way to politely get out of that shelter soon, she'd be the proud new mommy of a cuddly Chihuahua. With her work schedule, she didn't have much time for anything else. Hell, it'd been three years since her last date. It'd been even longer since her last mattress rodeo with a hunky guy she'd picked up at a bar back when she'd been feeling particularly wild and free. That feeling lasted a total of about four minutes—

basically, as long as the drunk jerk's erection lasted. Thankfully, she hadn't had to see him again. His performance had been less than stellar and hadn't really left her racing to find him for another romp.

"I'm sure he'd like anybody." Hayley laughed as she held the dog's tiny front paws in her hand. "Besides, he'd get lonely living with me and yeah, JoLynn Wheeler. Says she's from Paducah and I've noticed some quirky things about her, but nothing major and to be honest, something about her seems so familiar. I just can't place my finger on it. All I really care about is the fact that she handles distributing the loads and she has been a huge help fielding angry phone calls and threats from some faceless assholes."

A mischievous look in her friend's eyes warned her Savannah wasn't going to stop trying to get Hayley to take the dog with her. "Oh, really? Hmm…maybe you've met before." Sidestepping right back into puppy talk, "Ya know, Chihuahuas are very mild-mannered and easy to please. This one just needs some understanding. Besides, he's small enough that he could even go to work with you. Set him up a tiny bed in your office and I'll bet he'll sleep the day away while you're working. As for the threats, you still don't know who's behind them? Could it be Holt?"

"As far as meeting JoLynn before, I don't think so. I've never been anywhere really. There's just something about her eyes and the way she carries herself. Something about her brings out my protective side and yet, part of me feels like she's my younger, bratty and immature sister who wants to wear my clothes without permission. It's just an odd feelin'." She laughed, shaking her head at the notion. "Another no on Holt. Companies as big as Holt don't generally threaten with words. They throw their money around or undercut the rates on everything to steal the loads out from under everyone. That causes tension—big time. I'd love to have this dude, but what about when the drivers come in bitching about their fucked up loads? I wouldn't want to have him traumatized by their rants and ravings." Holding the dog up in front of her, she stared into the little guy's eyes. "You deserve a happy home, don't you? Right now, my office is as far from that as I can imagine."

"Have you ever seen a grown man turn to mush? All it takes is a baby or a small dog. Trust me. How about you try it out. Borrow him for the night or a few days and see what you think. Maybe you'll be able to figure out what he's wanting and if you bring him back, I'll know how to make him happy here until someone adopts him."

Borrowing him sounded like a fine idea. Sort of like test-driving a car. If he ended up being too much of a handful, she'd bring him back to her friend and she could at least say she tried. Besides, a handsome guy like this one to cuddle wouldn't exactly kill her.

"Okay. You've got a deal." I'll take him with me when I leave. "Now, how are you feeling?"

Savannah's grin spread ear-to-ear. "I'm good. It's been pretty warm outside this Spring but not enough to make me too uncomfortable. I haven't had too many Braxton-Hicks contractions, so I think I'll be on schedule with my due date. Only a few more weeks to go. I can't wait to meet this little one. Thankfully, when Ronnie gets here, Mason won't have to worry so much about me being alone."

"Is she moving here permanently? I think it'd be great if she did. She's a riot. How are she and Tex doing?"

After Savannah and Ronnie's house had been set on fire, Savannah had been kidnapped and Mason, being a true hero, had saved the day. Not long after, they'd gotten married at Mason's ranch. Hayley was introduced to Savannah and Ronnie at the rehearsal dinner and the three of them had become fast friends. Each of them from different walks of life and yet, they'd immediately formed a sisterhood of sorts. While Hayley kept Mason's trucks loaded, Savannah, who'd previously worked various jobs at a truck stop, was instantly immersed into the lifestyle by being married to a trucker and Ronnie was dating Tex, Mason's friend and fellow Asphalt Cowboy at Raisin' Kaine Trucking.

"Not sure. Depends, on work I suppose."

"Makes sense. I'm sorry about how things have been going."

Between shut down week and the fact that another trucking company was constantly cutting the rates, Mason's trucks were having a hard time staying loaded. Hayley felt like shit about that, but there wasn't anything she could do to fix it. The steel companies wanted to save money just like everyone else. All she could do was work her ass off to find Mason's guys more freight to make up for it. Some days were better than others were. Hopefully things would improve after the following week.

"Sweetie, it's not your fault. It's just how this business works. I understand it and I'm learning more each day. So don't beat yourself up over something that you can't control."

Hayley had trucking in her blood. Her father and grandfather had been long-haul drivers. Her father had been powerless against the call of the road, leaving Hayley and her mother alone, heartbroken and poor. Growing up, she knew her parents had never been happy. Before he'd left them, her dad was on the road all of the time and her mom had turned into a miserable person who shouted obscenities while her paranoia of Hayley's father cheating on her ran rampant. Vivian couldn't handle being a trucker's wife and it drove her to the edge of madness. So much so, that Hayley's mother had ended up institutionalized a few times. After her first rehabilitation and release, she'd channeled her sadness and anger into being a bar fly and a nuisance to the people in their very small town. The rest of Hayley's teenage years had been spent rescuing her mother from every bout of trouble she got herself into.

Watching what being a trucker's wife had done to her mother, and living through the feelings of worthlessness herself, Hayley swore she'd never date or marry a guy like her dad. But, she couldn't deny wanting and needing to be a part of the trucking world somehow. She was driven to do something for people, strangers or friends—doing something that mattered to someone.

If she could keep trucks loaded with freight that paid well enough, maybe she'd save a family. If drivers made enough money from fewer loads, that meant they'd be gone from home fewer days and that might make everything easier on families. In her head, it all made sense. Did she honestly think it made a huge difference? No. The only thing she knew for certain was that she'd never stop workin' her ass off for truckers and the people they loved--even if it was a thankless job ninety-nine percent of the time.

"I know. I just want to make a difference. Ya know?"

Savannah set down the bag of doggie kibbles and turned to face her friend. "Oh, Hales. You do make a difference. How could you think otherwise?"

Shrugging, she tucked a few flyaway chestnut waves that had escaped her ponytail behind her ears. "Well, I see you here on your own so often and now that steel is so slow, Mason will have to take loads that will keep him away from home more just to make up the lost income. I hope you can handle the stress of it all. It won't be easy. Those first state fair runs we're tryin' to land are gonna' be short jumps, but they're all across the country after next month. If it weren't for those assholes who keep swiping all of our contracts out from under us, things would be great."

"It'll be fine. I . . . we'll be fine. I'm a big girl and I can take care of myself and then some. Just take this coming week to relax and I think you'll be fine too." When Hayley tilted her head with a smile, she continued. "You need a break as much as those guys do. Dealing with all of them as much as you have to? I'd be goin' crazy. Add in Holt Trucking and you deserve a month-long vacation in Aruba." Savannah's laughter filled the small office and Hayley let herself enjoy that small, funny moment.

"True enough. I'm just sick of the shady shit. I've heard Holt's owner is buddy-buddy with all of the bigwigs and he takes them out to dinner, fishing on the company boat and other stuff that no one else can afford. He's the industry's biggest ass kisser. That's the real reason other offices and companies have caved to their rate slashing antics. It's all about the bottom dollar. How can I even hope to compete with that? I'm most worried about Mason, you and Aiden. I know how badly y'all need as much money as you can get your hands on right now."

"Money isn't everything." She smiled. "And if Sebastian would get his shit together, we'd have a huge weight lifted off of our shoulders. Everything else is easy."

Hayley and everyone else knew they had their hands full with Mason's brother, Sebastian, a.k.a., Romeo. Every dollar he made went to gambling, booze and women. Not long ago, Mason had no choice but to pay off another of Sebastian's huge gambling debts. If he hadn't coughed up the cash, the loan sharks would've kept Mason's equipment after Sebastian had offered it up in exchange for a miniscule loan with exorbitant interest. Between the bullshit with Sebastian and recent troubles with Savannah's ex, everyone involved had been under a mountain of stress.

"Maybe he'll wake up one day and realize how badly he's fucking up his life. And everyone else's. Don't give up, Savannah. He'll learn his lesson eventually. Aiden did. Maybe he can help somehow."

She knew firsthand how difficult it was for people to change. Aiden Hunt had had his share of troubles—many created by his own hands over the years. He was a nice enough guy and she'd never wish bad luck onto anyone, but there was something about Aiden that frustrated her more than most of the other drivers who came to her office. To top it all off, the man was walking sexuality. Thinking about him made her blood run hot and her body craved his touch.

With dark blonde hair that was just long enough to appear messy and disheveled., reminding her of her favorite country singer from Australia—the one who'd married a famous and gorgeous movie star. His firm, tight ass in those second-skin jeans that all hot cowboys wore made her want to stand him in a corner of her living room just so she could stare at that rear for hours at a time. An ass like that was a fine masterpiece—one she knew she'd never grow tired of seeing. When he spoke with the sexiest southern drawl she'd ever heard, it made her lose all rational thought. And if they were alone together for longer than a few minutes, she wanted to toss him onto any nearby surface and ride him until his body relaxed with sweet release. Aiden had a heart of gold and he scared the ever-living daylights out of her emotionally. She could lose herself in him and that couldn't happen. He was dangerous. Plain and simple.

In Hayley's eyes, his dark and jaded past couldn't tarnish the incredibly enticing package that Aiden Hunt was. Even his trucker handle got her hot and bothered. Phoenix. No handle had ever been truer to its owner. He was the king of climbing back to the top and he was trouble with a capital T. The kind of trouble that any other woman would gladly throw herself in front of just to say she'd danced with the Devil and survived it. That terrified Hayley because she knew Phoenix had the power to turn her into one of *those* women—the clingy, desperate for love kind of women. Her pride was something she refused to give up. Not even for a man like Aiden.

With one look, he could set fire to the walls she'd built around her heart, consuming her with pent up desire and deliver immediate satisfaction without even touching her. But, she could never tell him how she feels. They were friends . . . and the road would always be his number one lady. Finding a trucker like Savannah's husband, Mason, was like finding a company that paid a driver's entire fuel surcharge and Hayley felt that Aiden would never be able to balance a woman and his career as well as Mason did. Strange enough, Hayley acknowledged she was somewhat okay with that. She didn't really need a man in her life anyways. However, if she ever gathered enough nerve, she'd follow through on her sexual fantasies and give him a night, or day for that matter, that he'd never forget.

"From what Mason told me on the phone earlier, Aiden isn't exactly the guy to help us. Besides, he and Mason aren't seeing eye-to-eye right now. Aiden called him out in front of Tex when they stopped for coffee this mornin'. Needless to say, Mason is pretty pissed. Can't say that I blame him either."

Hayley listened to every word Savannah said as she explained what went down and hearing her speak of Aiden in a not-so-friendly way wasn't exactly making her happy at that moment. She couldn't put her finger on why, maybe she was tired, but badmouthing Aiden wasn't winning Savannah or Mason any brownie points with her. Hearing Savannah say that they expected Aiden to drag Sebastian out of the casino was beyond ridiculous and as his friend, she felt obligated to defend him.

"I know you love Mason and he's a great guy, but why would you want a recovering gambler to go into the casino? You'd rather Aiden jeopardized his recovery if it helped Mason's brother?"

"What do you mean?" A look of pure shock lit Savannah's face and Hayley knew she hadn't been told the entire story of what Aiden had been through and done in his past. "I didn't know about Aiden being a gambler. Well, former gambler. Oh my God."

"Yeah. He's been in way deeper than Sebastian has a time or two. Actually, more than a handful of times."

"Oh. It all makes so much sense now." Savannah rubbed her very prominent belly with one hand while pressing her other to the middle of her back as she arched in an effort to stretch her beautifully pregnant body. Being so close to her due date, Hayley figured she must be more uncomfortable than she was letting on and wished she could make everything better for her friend. "Does Mason know?"

"Of course."

"Why wouldn't he tell me?"

"Probably because it's not his story to tell. I don't know for sure. Aiden's had a really rough life and it's not exactly my place to say anything more. Besides, I don't know everything about him. We're great friends, but what I've heard from his own lips is all I can speak of."

To be honest, Hayley did know a lot more about him, but she'd never betray another person's trust, especially her good friend's. She hated gossip and always did her best to stay out of any drama. Her hands were already full enough each day with the disgruntled truckers who berated her when they didn't get the loads they wanted. She'd be damned if she'd add any fuel to the fire or be thrown into the mess between Aiden and Mason.

"Savannah, the way I see it, Sebastian has to fix himself. He has to want to change. No amount of bullying, threatening, ranting or raving will do that for him. It's an addiction and until he admits that, he will be a constant thorn in everyone's ass. Sorry, but it's the truth. I've seen my share of asshats at the office on a daily basis. One I'm currently dealing with is a guy who is always so furious every single day. When he can't load on his own time instead of the supplier's, the bitchin' begins. Some guys just don't have the common sense gene. Without that, they're worse than children who don't get their way." She bent down to scoop up the little Chihuahua who couldn't seem to leave her shoelaces alone. "My best advice? Don't get involved—if at all possible. Let the guys work it out themselves and bite your tongue when need be. No good ever comes out of gettin' in the middle of a bro-spat. It's all about who's got more muscles, bigger balls or who has the last word. No one wins."

"True." She watched as Savannah opened her mouth to say more, seemed to think better of it and pause for a moment. "Anyways, what are you gonna' name that little guy in your arms?"

"Nice swerve, girlfriend. You're just not gonna' let up, are ya?" Hayley chuckled as the tiny dog pressed his nose to hers.

"Why fight it? You're made for each other. I'll just go and gather his things. You and I both know you won't be bringing him back here."

Her friend laughed as she left her alone in the open waiting area holding the only guy that had managed to breach the hard-as-steel walls around her heart. The same walls that had remained intact for the past ten years despite being close to Aiden Hunt. "I'm such a sucker for gorgeous eyes and great hair. Prepare to be spoiled, stud puppy."

CHAPTER THREE

"Damn it. C'mon, big truck. Get outta' the way! Why would ya pull out in front of us and then hang out at fifty-five in a seventy?" Aiden let go of the CB mic and downshifted as he waited for the dick who'd cut him off to find the gas pedal and get movin'.

"What's your hurry, driver? Got a hot date or somethin'?" Another trucker piped up on the CB.

Grabbing the mic once again, Aiden rolled his eyes at the usual shit-tastic banter that occurred day and night. "Nah. I just know how to drive. These dickheads with their fancy, newer trucks get out here and slow the rest of us down 'cause they can't go but sixty-two tops. Motherfuckers think they're somethin' special just 'cause they've got a big company logo on their doors. Newsflash, a sticker is just a sticker and it don't make a trucker."

"I hear ya and agree. The key is to not let 'em know they get to ya. Then, ya blow their doors off and leave 'em behind."

"If the cocksucker would get back in the right lane, I would. Fuck. Who teaches these sonofabitches how to drive?"

Their conversation went on for another ten miles as they waited for the slower truck to move. At the last minute, the guy whipped his rig into the right lane, cutting off another truck in the process. Luckily, another driver was able to avoid hitting the asshole who then exited the interstate using the off ramp.

"Whoever gave that guy a license should have his head examined."

Drivers like that were a dime a dozen and they put everyone's lives at risk. Aiden didn't have a family to go home to, but nine out of ten truckers did. Most people didn't realize how difficult it is to stop or slow down quickly enough to avoid catastrophe. One wrong move and someone wasn't making it home. That old saying about 'an object in motion staying in motion' was absolute fact. Semis, especially semis with loaded trailers can't stop on a dime and every second of every hour out on the road was a gamble. Some days, Aiden wasn't sure it was worth the risk at all, but he'd never give up the high-stakes highway rodeo. He wasn't a quitter.

"Goddamn, that was close!" Another driver chimed in. "Someone should beat that dude's ass. I'm haulin' over eighty on the deck with these fuckin' coils. I'm already over the limit. If I'd have hit him, . . ."

The guy who'd been cut off stopped talking. Aiden could hear the fear and anger in the man's voice. It wasn't something any man was proud of, but they'd all been scared shitless at one time or another out on the road.

"I know, man. It's all right. Just take a deep breath."

"Yeah."

Aiden wanted nothing more than to line up every moronic driver and beat the shit out of 'em—even though he knew it wouldn't help. For every great trucker there were a thousand idiots behind the wheel. "Where ya headed, driver?"

"Kadence Steel. Damn, I can't wait to drop this shit off and get home. Gonna' hug my wife a little tighter when I get there. My daughter, too."

"Ten-four on that. This is my exit, travel safe, man."

"Back atcha', man."

Thankfully, Aiden had already delivered his last load for the week and he was looking forward to having the following week off. However, he had to admit—if only to himself, that it'd be nice to have someone waiting at home for him. For the most part, he embraced being on his own. No one nagging at him, nobody else to be responsible for and no commitments he'd run the risk of breaking by being devoted to that long ribbon of highway. Yet, a small percentage of the time, he longed for those very same things to be a part of his life. Most likely, because he'd never had them. Not really.

It was pretty difficult to find a woman he'd be able to spend more than an hour with when he spent twenty-four-seven between the lines. The only women he ever saw were working at the factories where he delivered, or waiting tables at the places he stopped to eat or they were already taken by men who'd found them first. Except Hayley Shaw. Just thinking of her made his chest tighten and his hands crave to touch those beautiful brown curls that always escaped the messy ponytail she pulled her unruly hair into. But she was off limits. They'd been friends for what seemed like forever. But if she ever gave him a chance . . . if he was the kind of man a woman like Hayley deserved, he'd spend the rest of his life lovin' her senseless. *If* he was that kind of guy and if he had anything substantial to offer her other than a past of failures and an uncertain future.

Shaking his head at the insipid notions his mind had wandered off to, Aiden's thoughts returned to work and his disagreement earlier in the week with Mason. They hadn't spoken since and Aiden realized that he wasn't exactly upset about it. All friends went through bullshit like that, but this time—he'd thrown a hard punch at Mason's ego and made direct contact. Who knew when he'd get over it? If it had been him, Aiden knew it'd take a while for the sting to subside.

Honestly, none of them had the time to worry about who'd hurt whose feelings. Their livelihoods were at stake. With other companies trying to stick their noses in on the freight, Mason and the others needed to focus on more than Sebastian and his fucked up antics and problems. He knew agents like Hayley Shaw and Mason's connections were working hard for all of them behind the scenes trying to grab local freight contracts. However, there was no guarantee that they weren't also working for the other companies like Mason's just as much. All of it was up in the air. Their best bet would be to get in on the state fair rides and hopefully, that was what Mason was focusing on instead of another bout of family drama with his addict of a brother.

Flicking his left turn signal on, Aiden downshifted, easing his rig onto the exit ramp as he headed towards home. His house wasn't anything special, but at least the small, two-bedroom home on a dead end road was his, free and clear. No one could take that away from him and he didn't plan on fuckin' things up again. He liked the bit of stability he'd finally found. Aiden did honest work for an honest living, leaving the gambling, booze and women far behind. Too bad he couldn't get rid of the memories from that time in his life.

Fifteen years ago, Aiden had been lucky enough to win the Ohio lottery which allotted him a total of four-hundred and fifty-thousand dollars. Being twenty years old and getting his hands on that much money was just another hill in a long path of slippery slopes. He'd won and lost plenty of times in the years before his big win. Mostly, he spent his nights in bleak and dark backrooms playing whatever card game he thought he could win.

Every dime he had made at his day job caring for race horses, went into the kitty each night.

When he won the lottery, it happened at the perfect time. He was in way too deep and owed an insane amount of cash to some guys who'd have been just as happy with taking each dollar out of his ass. He cashed that big-ass lottery check and hightailed it to eastern Kentucky and invested it into a ranch of his own—essentially fulfilling part of his dream as a young child. Owning a ranch, he could say he was a cowboy. For five years he did everything right; the horses he'd bought won often and won big. His investment had quadrupled in returns and that's when Aiden got greedy.

The lifestyle of owning winning derby horses, the booze, affluence and notoriety went to his head. And when his horses weren't competing the way they should be, a trainer turned him onto some nefarious methods to increase their chances on the track. He turned a blind eye to what his staff was doing. Told himself what he didn't know, he couldn't be held responsible for. The problem was—he did know and he continued to allow it to happen. The money was too good. His life was too grand. He was not only accepted; he became one of the elite with a bank account to rival the Old Money members in the upper rung of Kentucky's high society. Aiden was finally on top.

When federal investigators showed up after one of his best horses died during a race, shit got real and it got deep real fuckin' fast. They arrested his horse trainers, personal veterinarian and staff. All of his assets were frozen until the investigation and trial was over. When all was said and done, Aiden had lost everything. As a condition of his immunity deal, the sprawling, one-hundred-acre ranch, his horses, money and pride were stripped away quicker than a lot lizard's clothes on dollar night.

With that devastating reality check, Aiden was worse off than when he'd been destitute and alone right after leaving the orphanage. Back then, he hadn't known what it was like to have had anything worth being upset over. Losing the high life and home he'd built for himself in such a short time left him vulnerable to surviving in the only way he'd ever known in which he could make money quickly. After getting a job at a local super-store, back to gambling and filling the constant emptiness inside him he went. Aiden was born into having a losing hand. It'd taken him most of his life to accept it and he did the best he could with what he'd been given.

Most of the time, he messed up. He knew that and he'd hit rock bottom time and time again. But Aiden always got back up. That's how he'd come up with his handle. Like a phoenix rising from the ashes, he'd always find a way to get back on track. Meeting Mason and being given a chance at a normal life had been a blessing. More than he thought he deserved, really. Maybe someday he'd get far enough ahead again to just settle down and leave the road behind him. Or maybe he'd find a way to make Hayley see him as a man and not just a friend. She was the one woman he knew who was strong enough to handle his lifestyle and who'd enjoy travelin' around the country by his side. She might not admit it, but deep down Hayley needed to let loose and live a little. A man could dream and she belonged with him. He knew it.

Aiden looked around his property, watching as the cloudless blue sky perfectly reflected and highlighted the grass Kentucky was so well-known for. After travelin' to so many places in America, he'd never grow tired of seeing the rollin' hills of his beloved state. Standing on a hillside at the edge of his property, he could always find peace and whenever he needed a break from the highway hustle, that's where he allowed the magic of nature to wash over him—feeling what felt like a restoration of his soul and sanity. For a little while he could just . . . be.

It surprised him how much he simultaneously liked the alone time and longed for someone, no not just someone—Hayley Shaw, to share moments like these with. There was rarely a moment lately that she wasn't on his mind. Watching the sunset over the peaks and valleys of the Kentucky foothills was an amazing site to witness. In his opinion, everyone should take a deep breath once in a while and do more than exist. Maybe that made him a bit too sensitive—being a man and having reflective thoughts such as those. However, he'd learned that living hard and fast wasn't the only way to get through life. Sometimes, living meant slowing down and embracing the time on Earth given. Never a particularly religious man, Aiden could only say he believed everyone had a purpose. Someday, he knew he'd find his—even if he was alone.

CHAPTER FOUR

"Listen, Mason. I know you're all riled up but I'm workin' on it. Yes, I've spoken to Aiden, too. No, he didn't mention you. Look, as soon as I hear back from Donna in Laredo and Caroline up north, I'll let ya know. Just try to be patient. I've gotta go now. Give my love to Savannah."

Hayley set the phone back into its cradle and spun her office chair to look at the little man who'd not only captured her heart, but had also given her a much needed reality check. "Rocky, come 'ere, little guy." She patted her lap and the small Chihuahua quickly and eagerly launched himself into her arms. She held him close to her chest as he nuzzled against her neck. "I'd be lost without you, ya' know that?" The tiny pup snuggled deeper into her arms and Hayley embraced the small moment of quiet time.

Mason and his guys were all chomping at the bit. She couldn't blame them. They'd been out of work for two weeks and they were all antsy. She got it and also understood they all had expenses—expenses that demanded payment and didn't just vanish because there wasn't enough money. Hell, she didn't make money if the drivers weren't being loaded and Hayley knew how they felt. Sure, her expenses were nowhere near theirs, but the pressure of it all was getting to her. Their livelihoods and Mason's family depended on her. Having spent countless hours wishing for a magic solution to what was happening, she knew the problem of competing companies stealing their freight was far-reaching and she was at a loss as to what to do.

"Let's go for a walk. It's time to get outta here for a bit." Clipping the black leash to Rocky's skull and crossbones collar, they headed out. "Mail should be here. Maybe your treats have arrived." At the word 'treats', the pup picked up the pace, dragging her towards the mailbox at the end of the lane. "Whoa, little guy." He stopped, turning to look at her with those green eyes that had melted her heart almost a month ago and she spoke softly to him. "I know, I know. But we don't have to run. If the treats are in the box, they'll wait for us."

Sometimes, she felt stupid for talking to him like he was a person. But she knew he always understood every word she said to him. In some ways, he was like a human only with a lot of fur and four legs. Hell, he listened to her better than most of the people she'd met in her entire lifetime.

In just a few short weeks, she'd grown just as attached to Rocky as she had to the man she'd been friends with for what seemed like forever. And she realized just how much she'd been depending on Aiden to listen to her all of the time. With her little rockstar in her life, she now had someone else to help ease her worried mind and Hayley didn't feel the need to incessantly bug her longtime friend. He had a life of his own. Besides, sometimes she felt like the more she depended on Aiden, he might get the wrong idea. They were friends. Nothing more, right? A hot fantasy didn't make a real relationship.

Yeah, right. If you'd just stop holding onto that stupid rule as if it's a lifeline and give him a chance . . .

Regardless of how she felt about truckers and not dating them, her thoughts wandered to Aiden more and more as of late. The way he looked at her when they hung out or shared a dinner together—his green eyes full of devotion, as if she meant the world to him even though they both knew there were lines they couldn't cross.

There was the way he said her name or darlin' in that sticky, sweet southern drawl of his that had the power to throw her common sense out the window if she didn't make a conscious effort to keep her shit together. With the mantra "just friends" always running through her mind, she'd been lucky to keep things on a platonic level. Without it, she'd run the risk of leaping into unknown territory and with it was the chance she'd be burned. Hayley didn't know if she'd ever be ready for such a gamble, but the desire and need within her was close to overflowing.

She thought back to words her father liked to say on the rare occasion he'd call her from the road. "Hayley-bird," his special nickname for her because as a child when he still lived with them, she'd follow him around the house on weekends parroting his every word and move.

"You need to learn how to fly. Get out there and live. Stop guarding your heart. It's not just yours. It belongs to someone else out there in the world and you'll never find them if you stay in your nest. Promise me you'll fly someday." Though his voice was one of a man who'd lived his life on the road—gruff, he couldn't hide any emotion or love beneath his raspy, matter-of-fact tone. She carried those words and the way he'd said them with her.

Hayley promised she'd do as he said. However, all these years later after the nickname began, she still hadn't summoned up the nerve to spread her wings and see what the world had in store for her. She liked her nest, as her father called it. In it, she was safe, but deep down, Hayley also knew her father was right. He'd always been right. Somewhere out there was the person her heart was destined for. Whether they broke it or not, she needed to find a way to let go of her fears and embrace whatever living her life had in store for her. Lately, working out of an office just wasn't cutting it.

With a deep breath, she snapped out of her reverie and proceeded to walk towards the end of the half-mile-long driveway. The red barn replica mailbox was stuffed with letters and a small package wrapped in plain, brown paper and addressed to her personally with no return address.

"That's weird. Usually they send your treats with our business name on the front." Rocky tilted his head side-to-side and with a wag of his tail sat up on his hind legs, waving his front paws, begging for a treat. "Not yet. Let's finish our walk."

The air was dry and humid. Just the way she liked it. Hating the cold, she reveled in the heat of Kentucky springs and summers. Waking up each day to the warmth of the sun on her face was like Christmas to her. It was when she felt the most like herself. As she and Rocky walked along the dirt path back to her office, she tilted her face to the sky, loving the heat upon her skin. Although it was ninety-two with a heat index of one hundred, Rocky didn't seem to mind being outside in the humidity. Wherever she went, he happily trotted by her side and for that, she was extremely grateful. He was an easy guy to train and love.

Once they were inside the large office, the cool central air was both a small relief and chilling as goosebumps rose on the bare, tanned flesh of her arms. Most days, she wore whatever was comfortable yet nice enough for running her own office. That day, she'd opted for a sleeveless navy blouse adorned with southwestern inspired embroidery along the hem. A pair of denim capris and a pair of plain, white canvas shoes completed the look. Running late, Hayley had been in such a hurry that she'd left the house without grabbing her favorite hoodie that she usually brought with her each day just in case she felt chilly or in the event that it rained. So, she removed the ponytail holder from her brunette locks and rubbed her arms, mentally willing her body to adapt to the sudden temperature change.

"Here you go, boy. A fresh bowl of water." Hayley gave him the cool liquid and unhooked the leash from his collar before making her way to the pile of mail she'd dropped upon her desk when they'd returned. Opting for satisfying her curiosity, she plucked the small package off of the wooden surface to examine it more closely.

"So strange." Without giving a thought to the fact that it could be from whomever had been sending her veiled threats via text message and voicemail, she tore into the brown paper, making quick work of it.

"Shit!" Dropping the contents onto her desk and plucking her cell phone off of the same surface, she called the one person she knew she could always trust.

"Hey, darlin'. What's up?"

"Aiden, please get out here to the office."

"What's wrong? Are you hurt?"

"No. Just…please, please hurry."

Ending the call, she scooped Rocky into her arms and went outside to wait for her friend to arrive. "It'll be okay, buddy. I promise it'll be okay."

CHAPTER FIVE

Gravel and dust created a tornado of debris as Aiden tore out of his driveway—not caring if the small rocks chipped the paint of his new pickup. Hayley needed him. The urgency and fear in her voice had shaken him to his core. In all the years he'd known her, she had never sounded that way.

"Fucking lights!" Not one of the stoplights through town was on his side and Aiden cursed himself for not taking the backroads. "Screw it." He mashed the gas as he sped through the busy burg. Part of him not caring that he could very well be pulled over any minute by one of the sheriffs and the other part of him hoping they would so he could bring them with him to his friend's office.

Once he made it through the last of the intersections, Aiden barely let off the gas as he cranked the wheel hard to the right. The winding gravel roads that led him to reach Hayley would've been tricky to maneuver at such high speeds if he weren't accustomed to flying down them so often. If need be, Aiden could get to the office blindfolded. Past the fields of immature field corn and beans, he could see the top floor of the building he visited at least three times a week for the past five years. The dark green metal roof and cedar walls teasing him with the illusion of being able to reach out and touch them from where he was. The winding roads, peaks and valleys of the rural area told him otherwise. It seemed like no matter how hard he pressed the accelerator, he couldn't get there fast enough.

"Hold on, babe. I'm almost there."

As the minutes ticked by like hours, Aiden drummed his thumb on the black steering wheel while worry and fear rushed through his mind at lightning speed. If it were anyone else who needed his help, he'd be able to find a way to stay calm. But not where Hayley was concerned. No one messed with her. All he wanted was to shield her from everything bad in the world . . . for her to be with him, by his side. If someone was out to get her, he'd make them pay.

Taking into consideration the shady operations of other steel industry companies, he was already on edge. Plus, she had been under tremendous stress lately and though she claimed her new dispatcher, JoLynn, was a huge help—Aiden knew there was only so much JoLynn had the experience to do. She wasn't anywhere close to being as great as Hayley was. On a side note, something about the new employee rubbed him the wrong way. She'd arrived too conveniently—almost immediately after a help wanted ad had been placed and her overeager willingness to please Hayley was just very unnerving to Aiden.

Arriving at the office in a cloud of dust, sliding sideways as he slammed on the brakes, he shoved the gear shift into park before throwing open the door to jump out of the lifted beast of a truck.

She stood by her pickup, holding her new pup and ran into his arms. "Darlin'?" Aiden rubbed her back as he held her close to him and she pressed her body deeper into his. "Babe, I love having every curve of you against me, believe me, I do. But your pup is gonna get smashed and honestly, I won't want to let you go if I hold you any tighter."

"Damn." She muttered and quickly stepped out of his embrace. "I'm sorry. I don't know what came over me, Aiden." The sudden rosy tint to her cheeks and the way she turned her head away let him know she was embarrassed. That one moment made his heart swell. His friend was a whirlwind of everything he'd ever wanted in a woman; shy, funny, beautiful and strong. God help him, she was perfect in his eyes.

He watched as she planted kiss after kiss atop the tiny dog's head as she avoided eye contact with Aiden. In that moment, he couldn't deny he was a little more than jealous of Rocky. "No need to be sorry. What happened out here? Whose ass do I need to kick? And don't say no one's because whoever got you this upset surely deserves my boot in their ass. Sideways—if you ask me."

With a sigh, she muttered, "I don't know. A small package arrived a little while ago. It's in there on the desk and I think I should call the cops at this point. I don't know what else to do, Aiden."

Goddamn it. Walking over to her, Aiden lightly grasped her shoulders. "You stay here. If anyone who's not to supposed to be here comes, just yell. Okay?"

He charged up the steps leading to the door of her main office, his boots thundering on the wooden planks all the way into the building. On the desk lay what was left of the shredded brown packaging and a small, white stuffed dog. Beside it was a label from a well-known rat poison company. "Mother fucking sick bastards."

Aiden scrubbed one hand over his face, willing himself to stay as calm as possible. He couldn't go back out there half-cocked and ready to rip someone apart, but now these fuckers were making shit personal. Reaching into his pocket, he retrieved his cell phone and dialed Sheriff Baynes' personal number. From this point forward, all threats—vocal or tangible were going to be documented with the authorities. Shit just got real. He'd be fucked and fire-hosed before he'd let any harm come to Hayley or Rocky.

"Yeah." The older man on the other end of the line answered in his usual gruff voice. "Sheriff Baynes, here."

"Hey, man. It's Phoenix. You got time to come out to Hayley Shaw's office? We've got . . . situation that needs your attention."

"What kind of situation? An emergency? If so, dial the department. I'm watchin' the game."

"Baynes, there's no game on tonight. And it's a situation I'd like to keep quiet. If ya know what I mean."

"Fine. It's a game I recorded last season on the DVR. But, whatever. I'll be there as soon as I can. Bunch of needy bastards."

Aiden laughed at the old man as he hung up the phone. From what he'd heard, Sheriff Baynes, in all of his sixty-plus years, had always been the same. No nonsense, a bit self-centered and a real stickler for the law. Knowing he was almost ready to retire saddened Aiden. The guys at the department these days weren't the least bit interested in actual justice. They were more concerned with monthly speeding ticket quotas and they all had hard-ons for Mason's trucking company. At least once a month, one of them tried busting Mason's guys' balls. Not having Baynes around would make things worse on truckers heading in or out of town than they already were.

The sound of gravel crushing under tires had Aiden rushing outside to see who'd shown up. "It's JoLynn, Aiden. No need to be concerned."

"You called her?" He moved closer to Hayley. Standing to her left, their thighs almost touching, Aiden could feel the heat of her skin from mere inches away.

Damn. What he wouldn't give to have her in his arms again. She fit so perfectly, so right.

"No. She called me. Perfect timing, huh?"

"Yeah, perfect." Again, he felt something wasn't right where JoLynn Wheeler was concerned.

"Hey, guys." JoLynn slithered out of her low-to-the-ground sports car and patted at the wrinkles on her shirt. When she closed the door of her car, Aiden couldn't help but notice how similarly she and Hayley were dressed again. Every damn day it seemed as though they were coordinating their clothing and it was fucking weird.

"Thanks for comin' out, sweetie. But I told you Aiden and I had it covered."

"The sheriff is on his way. Unless you have somethin' to tell him, he probably won't need to speak to you, JoLynn."

"Look at you, Aiden. Callin' in the big man in uniform. I figured a big, tough and" JoLynn looked up and down every inch of Aiden's six-foot-plus frame, "dependable guy like you would've just tracked down who's doin' this by yourself. Surely, you're the man to do it. But, actually, I'd love to stay here with you and speak to him about the past threats. After all, I'm the one who's always here with Hayley."

Aiden looked at the blonde woman, sizing her up and measuring her words. He couldn't tell if the woman was hitting on him or claiming territory over Hayley. Or both. Either way, somethin' about her stunk to high heaven and it wasn't just the perfume she obviously bathed in. Hayley might trust the woman, but Aiden knew a skank when he saw one. JoLynn was definitely not who she claimed to be.

"JoLynn, I'm so grateful you're here. Without you by my side this past few months, I'd have never made it through all of this. Thank you for wanting to add to the report." Hayley smiled at her employee and when she turned away, Aiden caught of glimpse of another side of JoLynn. He couldn't explain it, but it seemed like she'd briefly sneered at Hayley. Not the kind of behavior you'd expect to see from a woman who supposedly wanted to help.

For the moment, he tucked away his personal opinions about the woman and cleared his throat when he spotted the sheriff haulin' ass in his Jeep towards them. The familiar sounds of Conway Twitty's voice blasting through the speakers in the old man's vehicle gave Aiden a grin. It was nice to know that people still knew how to appreciate great music. He, himself preferred classic country and hair bands. Knowing it was an odd combination, eclectic if you will, of genres for a man to like, but he didn't care. Hell, Hayley liked alternative rock, country and metal. Watching her headbang to some Metallica or Danzig was just one of the things he loved about her.

"Okay. What the hell's goin' on and why the fuck am I out here in the middle of nowhere on such a hot damn day?"

"Howdy, Baynes. Thanks for comin'." Aiden reached out to shake the man's hand.

"Knock it off with that shit. Whatcha' tryin' to shake my hand for? I ain't out here for formalities. Let's get inside before we all fry up like sidemeat out here. For shit's sake, don't y'all have any common sense? Give me that pup. I'll take him inside where he can relax. Y'all have probably been out here too long all ready. Bunch of morons."

Aiden, Hayley and JoLynn followed the sheriff into the office building. None of them uttering a word and all of them muffling their laughter. Life without Sheriff Baynes and his sunny disposition would surely be boring once he retired.

CHAPTER SIX

"Seems you've got an interesting situation on your hands, little lady." Sheriff Baynes picked up a pencil from Hayley's monstrous desk and used the eraser end to move the small stuffed animal, looking it over with concern furrowing his brow. "Start from the beginning and tell me everything."

He removed his hat and seated himself in a wooden chair that sat opposite from the desk. Rocky launched himself onto the older gentleman's lap and immediately planted his paws on the man's chest before covering his face in a deluge of sloppy kisses. "Yes, boy. Sit here and be good." Needing no further instruction, the small dog plopped down and stared at Hayley with a look that told her she should be jealous of him finding a new pal.

"Such a ham. Okay, Sheriff. The threats began a few months ago. Right around the time steel freight began to slow down, we started to get texts and phone calls from trucking companies and their drivers. Each one telling us we'd be shoved out of the area or they had agents who could run circles around me. The best one had to be when they said a woman like me had no business telling men how to run or where to run. Honestly, I laughed it off at first. Men will be men, ya know?"

"Sure." The sheriff tilted his head back a bit and rubbed Rocky's head as he listened.

"Well, it became entirely too much to deal with so I sent out a notice that I was looking for a new dispatcher. Dealing with the menacing calls, texts, voicemails and trying to run my business while keeping trucks loaded wasn't working. JoLynn was the first to show up for an interview and with her experience, I hired her on the spot. Since that day, she's been the one dealing with the ridiculous behavior and she's shielded me from most of this damn nonsense. I've been breakin' my back tryin' to land accounts for Mason's guys and with them all being on shut-down the past few weeks, having her here has been a huge blessing. There are a shit-ton of drivers who are even more worked up now that work has come to a halt."

"So, who do you think is doin' this? Any one person or group of people in particular?"

"To be honest, until today I thought it was this one trucker who's always pissed. But once I opened that package," she pointed to the disgusting passive-aggressive threat on her desk, "I knew it was something more sinister and personal. Who does something like that? What do they want from me? Threatening an innocent puppy?" The tears she'd been suppressing finally broke free and she sobbed into her hands.

JoLynn and Aiden moved to opposite sides of Hayley's shaking frame. JoLynn wrapped her arms around her. Out of the corner of her eye, she saw Aiden grow tense and step away.

"JoLynn, tell me what you've been dealin' with." Sheriff Baynes gently placed Rocky on the floor and withdrew a small notebook and pen from the pocket of his starched, khaki uniform shirt.

"Well, like poor Hayley told you. These guys call here and always from unlisted numbers. They've threatened to run her out of town and have called her every name in the book. I try to keep most of it from her."

"Why's that?" He scribbled a few things down in his notebook and waited for her to continue.

"She's super busy and stressed out. My job is to make her life easier." JoLynn rubbed Hayley's shoulder. "She's become more than my boss—she's my friend, Sheriff. I care about her a lot—like a sister. Why would I want to tell her these horrible men have threatened bodily harm called her despicable names and have threatened to burn the place down with her and Rocky in it?"

Hayley gasped in shock. "Are you serious? They've said those things? You should've told me so that I could be more alert. Who knows what could've been in that package today!"

JoLynn began sobbing, "I'm so sorry, Hales. I just wanted to do my job and keep you from worrying. I was just trying to," she wiped at her nose, "help you. I didn't think I was doin' anything wrong."

Hales? Now she's using the nickname that only her inner circle called her.

Hayley tucked the thought away and tuned back into the conversation at hand.

"For fuck's sake. How damn incompetent are ya? She or Rocky could've been . . ." Aiden spoke up, shocking Hayley with his irritation.

"Aiden! She's clearly upset. Look, I'm sorry I yelled at you, JoLynn. I know you were just doing what you thought was best for me." Hayley held her friend until she calmed down.

"Sheriff, what are you gonna do about all of this?" Aiden crossed his arms over his middle and Hayley could see anger bouncing off of him in waves.

"Since the packaging has been shredded to bits and the items inside have been touched by Hayley, I doubt we'll get any useful print off of any of it. As for the threats by phone, I can have someone set up a trace."

"That won't be necessary, sir." JoLynn piped up. "If they call or text again, I'll call you or the department right away. Aren't you getting ready to retire? I'll have one of the other guys come out here if anything else happens. Promise. I'll spend night and day keeping my friend and this adorable pup," she knelt down to pat Rocky's head and jerked her hand away when he growled at her, "safe."

Sheriff Baynes rolled his eyes and with an exasperated sigh, "Don't know why y'all called me. Seems you'll handle it all just fine by yourselves. Aiden? Let's leave these two women to get back to whatever it is they do around here. Come outside with me." Placing his wide brimmed hat atop his balding head, the sheriff tipped it at her and JoLynn as he made his way to the door. "Bye, ladies."

"Sheriff Baynes? I'm sorry you had to come all the way out here. But thank you for doing so. I truly appreciate it."

"Yeah, whatever. Stay safe, little lady." He lowered his voice to whisper. "If you need me, you know you can call me anytime. Got it?"

Hayley nodded with a smile. "Thank you again. Be safe heading home."

She watched as he and Aiden went outside. "Thank you for being here, JoLynn. I'm really sorry I snapped at you."

"No worries. We're all under a lot of stress lately." Her flippant words revealed no sign of the crying woman who'd been standing in her place only moments ago. Instead, JoLynn was all business with an air of indifference as she fiddled about gathering the threatening mail. "I'll just take care of this for you."

"Sure. Thanks."

For a brief moment, JoLynn's sudden change in temperament struck Hayley as odd, but she shrugged it off as being overly suspicious again. Did she honestly need to be so paranoid about how everyone around her was acting? JoLynn adored her and sure, she was quite quirky but she knew the woman's heart was always in the right place. She admired the fact that JoLynn Wheeler was a strong woman when need be. In fact, she reminded Hayley a lot of herself in some ways. They could be sisters had it not been for their differences in hair color.

JoLynn left the building, headed toward the dumpster outside and Hayley returned her attention to the two men who'd exited only moments before. "Why would he want to speak to Aiden privately? It had nothing to do with him." Mumbling under her breath, she couldn't help but notice the look of concern on both of their faces as she spied on them through her small office window.

"There. Out of sight, out of mind." JoLynn walked into the room, rubbing her hands together. "Now, I can get back to work."

"Actually, I think Rocky and I are gonna head home. I really need a break from this place."

"Oh, sweetie. I completely understand. Don't you worry. I'll tidy things up, make a few phone calls and make sure everything is secure before I leave for the evening. You just go on home and get some rest. This entire ordeal must be so hard on you."

"Yeah. Come on, Rocky. Let's get outta here. I'm so done with this place and everything that goes with it."

"Maybe you should take a few days off. Ya know? Just to relax. Spend some time with Rocky. It's not like we're crazy busy anyways."

"Nah. I'll be here tomorrow. This business is my responsibility."

"Sure. Just know I'm here to watch over things if you change your mind. Okay, honey?"

"Thanks. See ya tomorrow."

The conversation between Aiden and the sheriff came to an immediate halt as soon as she stepped foot out onto the porch of her building. "Gentlemen, thanks for comin' out. We're headin' home. If you need me, you know where and how to reach me."

"Want me to give ya a lift, Hales? Since we're not workin' tomorrow, I can even bring you back here in the mornin'."

"Thanks, Aiden. I'll be all right. I just need to be alone for a while. It's time for some serious cuddlin' with my little man here. Talk to you later." Being around Aiden while she was feeling vulnerable and on edge was the last thing in the world she needed. Yet, part of her would also love a movie night and binge eating with her handsome friend.

"Sweetheart, I'd really feel better if you let me drive you or at least follow you." Aiden's gaze pierced right through the brave front she'd been trying to hold onto and she needed to get out of there quickly before he and Sheriff Baynes saw every feeling she'd been hiding from him came rushing to the surface.

Rising up on her tiptoes, Hayley planted a kiss on her friend's cheek and turned to shake the sheriff's hand.

"You know better than that. He gets a kiss and ya think I want a silly handshake? How long have we known each other? Come 'ere." The burly man wrapped her in his arms and held her tight for a moment. Be safe, hear me?"

"Yes, sir." He squeezed her until she giggled and when he finally released her, the sheriff bent down to rub Rocky's head.

"Take care of her. She's pretty special to us. Hear me?"

Rocky snorted in response, wagging his tail as she carried him to her pickup. She never thought she'd have one man that cared about her. How did I get lucky enough to end up with three of you, short stuff?"

CHAPTER SEVEN

Aiden waited until Hayley was in her truck, out of earshot and finally on her way home. Checking behind him to be sure JoLynn wasn't lurking, he continued the conversation with the sheriff. "I'm worried about her."

"I know, son. So am I. But, she's a big girl and we can't tell her what to do. At least she has help here at the office."

"Some fucking help." Aiden muttered. "With friends like that . . ."

"Friends like what, Aiden?" JoLynn's perfume smacked him in the face before she stood by his side.

"Jesus! Warn a person. Ya need to wear a bell around your neck or somethin'. We were just talkin' about someone Hayley used to know."

"Ah, I see. Well, she's never mentioned any friends to me and I know everything about her. So, that person must not be very relevant to her life now." She raised long, slender fingers to her wavy blonde locks and twirled some strands as she spoke. When Hayley did it, it was enduring. Watching JoLynn do it made him nauseous.

"You could say that."

"Well, I'm headed home. Aiden, remember what we talked about and I'll get ahold of you if anything pops up. Bye, JoLynn. It was nice to meet you."

"You too, sheriff. You're just the sweetest thang!"

The damn woman couldn't decide if she had an accent or not. One moment she was speaking without it, the next, she sounds like she belonged in an episode of Alice playing the part of Flo. Aiden knew for a fact that anyone born and raised in Paducah had an accent that was as clear as the shine on the chrome of his truck was. Too many things about the woman rubbed him the wrong way. Maybe it was just jealousy that Hayley had a new friend, but he didn't think so. His gut told him something was truly wrong.

"Bye, Baynes. I'll be in touch."

The sheriff climbed into his Jeep, giving both of them a mock salute and a wave as he headed down the long winding road.

"Well, I best be goin' too. See ya later. Be sure to have everything locked up tight, JoLynn."

"Aiden? Wait. Couldn't you stay here for a little while? Just until I'm finished. I really don't want to be here alone right now." She placed slender palms on his chest and looked at him with large doe eyes.

Leave. Just leave. "Sure. As long as it won't take you too long. I've got somethin' to take care of."

"Yay! Thanks so much. You're a peach! I feel so much safer with a big, handsome man like you around." She flung her arms around his neck, bringing their lips in dangerous proximity to each other's.

"Yeah, well. Let's just get inside so you can finish your work." He untangled himself out of her arms and stepped back.

A flicker of irritation lit the woman's face, but it was gone in an instant. "Let's get to it then."

With one last cursory glance around the property, he followed her inside.

"Just make yourself comfortable. I just need to tidy up and organize some files. Hayley has so much on her plate all ready and this office is in such a state of disarray. If you ask me, I think she needs a vacation. I can't stand seeing all of this clutter."

"Well, she does have a lot goin' on." He watched as JoLynn went out of her way to bend over, giving him a nice full view of her curvy ass in those tight denim capris. He refrained from rolling his eyes and instead, cleared his throat.

"Oh. I bet you're thirsty, aren't you? Well, you sit right there and I'll get you a nice cold glass of sweet tea."

Again with the fucking fake accent! She sashayed out of the room and into the kitchen Hayley had remodeled when she'd first opened up the place. In there was everything a driver could want or need. She kept it fully stocked with drinks, snacks, meat to make a full meal on the large stove and she'd even brought in a deep freeze last year that was always restocked by the local butcher. She took care of her guys like no other agent he'd ever known. They were all lucky to have her in their lives.

"Here ya go, sweetheart. Oh!"

JoLynn fell towards him, the glass of tea flying through the air, sending the cold beverage towards him at lightning speed. Before he could react, he was covered in the sticky-sweet liquid and JoLynn was on her knees in front of him.

"Oh, I'm just so very sorry, Aiden. Let me clean you up."

She placed her hands on his legs, giving his wet lap a long lust-filled look before using his thighs as leverage to stand in front of him. The woman looked as though she'd devour him in an instant!

What the actual fuck?

"No. It's fine. Really. Are you okay? You're the one who took a tumble."

"It was nothin', sugar. Aren't you the sweetest. Concerned about me when I've ruined your white shirt. You should really get that off . . . so it can soak." She bit on the end of a long, purple painted nail, her tongue darting out to touch the tip for more than a second too long and making Aiden even more at a loss for words than he already was.

If that were even possible. Awkward doesn't even begin to describe this moment.

"It's old. I can use it for rags at the shop."

Highly uncomfortable and not from the sugary tea that had permeated the denim and cotton covering his crotch. Though, sticky, sugar coated balls weren't the best feeling, being around JoLynn and her . . . womanly wiles was even worse. He'd never had a woman so blatantly throwing herself at him. He doubted she'd act this way in front of Hayley.

So, what is she really up to?

"See? That's just one more thing that needs attention around here. That damn rug! Honestly, I think Hayley's off her game. Really, Aiden. I'm very worried about her." She traced the collar of his shirt with the same purple nail tip she'd seductively had in her mouth only moments before.

He wasn't sure if the woman was after him or out to get Hayley. One thing he did know was that he needed to put as much distance between JoLynn and himself quickly. Unfolding himself from the chair, he stood and stepped to his left.

"I'm just gonna use the bathroom to get some of this tea off of me. Try to finish your work so we can leave. Okay?"

"Sure. You go get cleaned up, sugar. I'll be right here when you get back."

Of course ya will be.

She had work to do. But the way she said it made his skin crawl in revulsion. Making his way to the second floor, Aiden passed the walls of framed awards Hayley had received for being 'Agent of the Month' and 'Agent of the Year' for the past three years running. She was damn good at her job, but she never flaunted it outside the office. She was a humble and hardworking woman—never flashy or gaudy. She had class and integrity. If he added up everything he loved about her, the number would go on infinitely. There wasn't a thing about her he didn't like. Well, except for that one rule. However, come to think of it. If she wasn't willing to date him, she wasn't willing to date any other truckers either. That was good enough for him. For the moment.

Someday, he'd find a way to make her see him as more than a friend—more than just another trucker she loaded. Aiden would show her the real man he was and the man he could be for her. She deserved the world and if he had to give up being on the road to give her everything she'd ever wanted, by God, he'd do it. The road wasn't always so great anyways. But for now, while he was off work along with everyone else, he was going to make sure Hayley and Rocky stayed safe from whomever was out there that had some fucked up axe to grind with her. Someone had to take care of her and his gut told him JoLynn was only looking out for herself and whatever she could get out of anyone she could manipulate—if she hurt people on the climb up, he doubted she'd give two fucks.

Making quick work of washing up as best as he could, Aiden dried off and headed back downstairs. JoLynn was once again bent over. This time she was watering all of the plants Hayley kept around the office. Before reaching the room, he heard her speaking to someone. Since he hadn't heard anyone come into the office, he surmised she was on her cell phone. He waited in the shadows of the hallway and listened.

In a low and very different tone than he'd heard from her that day, she said "I don't care. Get it done. Make it happen. I'm tired of the games. This shit needs to end soon. I can't take much more of this. You were paid and I want the job done. You have one week. If you want things to go in your favor, I highly suggest you get your shit together."

Aiden moved into the kitchen, holding his breath and made sure he'd memorized every word she said. What the fuck was the woman up to? After he waited another minute or so, there was complete silence. He walked over to the refrigerator and grabbed a bottle of water, making as much noise as he could before he turned around to head back toward the office.

"Hey there, handsome." The accent was back. "All cleaned up and ready to go?"

"Absolutely. Who was that on the phone? Hayley?"

"Nah, sugar. Just some silly telemarketer."

"At this hour? It sounded more serious than that. Your voice was . . . um . . . different."

Waving his comments away with a flippant hand gesture, "Don't you worry your handsome head about it. I took care of him."

Oh, he was worried and no sugar-coating from the fake woman was going to dissuade him, but he digressed. Filing away even more of what he'd observed that day, he let the conversation die. "I'll leave you to lock up and I'll follow you home. Just to make sure you get there safely."

"Aww, sugar. You truly don't have to do that. I'll be just fine."

"I insist, JoLynn." Gagging on his own words, he continued. "A woman can't be too careful and considering that you and Hayley have been the victims of some truly awful threats, I wouldn't be a man if I let you go home unescorted."

Damn. Being nice never sickened him so much. But this was for Hayley. He needed to remember that.

A look of satisfaction crossed the woman's features. She obviously thought she had him where she wanted him. Licking and smacking her full, pink lips, "Well, if you insist. Maybe you'll join me for a nightcap when we get there."

"Maybe." Aiden knew what he had to do. Finding out where JoLynn lived was going to be the beginning. As a former con and gambler, he knew another con artist when he saw one.

JoLynn sashayed around the office. After setting the phones to go straight to voicemail, she switched off the computer monitors and did a quick sweep of the entire place. "All set, sugar. Windows are locked, place is as tidy as Hayley likes it so she won't throw a fit tomorrow." Even though they were the only two people in the building, she lowered her voice to a whisper. "You know those tiny tantrums she throws." With a shrug, she continued, "Hayley's a bit of a neat freak which is why her behavior and lack of attention to detail lately, surprises me. Must be all that stress she's always sayin' she's under." When Aiden didn't respond, she feigned indifference, ushering him outside and slid her key into the deadbolt after she closed the door behind them. "Let's go, sugar. I can't wait to show you my . . . place."

After they'd climbed into their respective vehicles, Aiden let out a long, deep breath and prayed Hayley wouldn't be pissed he was following JoLynn home. But he had to. Aiden knew for a fact that everything about JoLynn's demeanor and behavior made him believe her words before locking the office doors were the truest things to come out of her mouth in a very long time.

Whether she liked it or not, the evening wasn't going to end the way she hoped. Aiden wasn't about to become one of Hayley's things that JoLynn acquired. He sure had a feeling that the woman was after more than a nightcap with him. Everything about the woman was firing off alarms inside his head. Aiden planned to gather as much info as he could about the woman before he went to Hayley with his suspicions. He could only hope he wouldn't be too late to stop whatever the conniving snake had in store for his friend.

Making their way through town was easier at that late hour. Evening traffic didn't congest the streets as much as mid-day did and though JoLynn took many twists and turns heading out towards the Sand Creek area, Aiden had no problem staying with her. There were other, more direct ways she could've taken and her attempts at confusing him were confusing, juvenile and futile. Hadn't she been thrilled that he'd be following her home? She obviously didn't know that he wasn't a rookie driver and could navigate anywhere in the country. There was no way in hell that dragging him around the backroads of his own stomping grounds was going to deter or frustrate him.

"We can play cat and mouse all night, lady. You're not losin' me." Grumbling, Aiden mentally tucked away more opinions about the devious woman who was leading the way.

The fact that she was swerving and weaving all over the road was unnerving for him and it pissed him off when she nearly collided with other vehicles three different times.

"Christ! The woman must be finger-fucking her phone. Or she's absolutely fucking crazy. God help us all if she drives like this all the time. It's a good way to get everyone killed."

He should know. Every day and night he was surrounded by idiots who couldn't make it a mile without being attached to their cell phones in one way or another. Too many people didn't understand the importance of paying attention to the road. All it took was a split second to change the lives of many and the outcome was never a good one.

Once they arrived at a half-mile long lane leading to a dilapidated farmhouse out on Cutter's Road, he was a bit surprised. For years, he'd believed the home to have been abandoned. Aiden slowed his pickup to a crawl. The dips and potholes along the dirt path were big enough to swallow the car JoLynn was driving. However, she maintained a steady pace and bounced over the rough terrain, dodging and weaving around very few of the ruts and that left Aiden shaking his head again at her carelessness.

"She'll be lucky if there's anything left of that car once she gets to the house. What the fuck? Thank God that woman spends most of her time behind a desk. But God help the people who are out on the roads at the same time she's on them."

He approached the house as the sun was setting and parked his truck off to the left side of JoLynn's dusty red car. Off in the distance, the horizon behind the farm reminded him of the cotton candy one of the many sets of foster parents had bought for him one year at a local carnival. The sickly sweet taste had been something he'd never forget. Maybe because it had been the first and only time he'd ever eaten the sugary confection. Or maybe it was a memory forever etched into his mind because they'd returned him to the orphanage the next day—saying he wasn't like normal kids. According to them, all kids loved cotton candy, the fair and of the things they couldn't get him to be enthusiastic about.

He'd never been fake—not for them or anyone else. It seemed as though his entire life had been spent holding onto that feeling inside of him—the one that told him to be true to himself and follow his own path. Yet everyone he had ever met up until he'd met Hayley had all shown him a false side of themselves until an event came about forcing them to show their true colors. Once a lesson had been learned about those people, he moved on—drifting away from them and all the better for it.

Day after day, it was becoming more difficult to deal with fakery and bullshit of the steel industry. Whether it was supposed friends, drivers or companies, he was beginning to feel the burn out all drivers experienced once in a while. Now he was dealing with one of the most unbelievable people he'd ever met. No, he didn't have to be in this situation, but he chose to be—needed to be in order to protect his friend. His past of being a successful gambler was coming in handy. His instincts were screaming that JoLynn was as fake as the long, blonde extensions attached to her head. The woman was the complete and total opposite of Hayley. So why did he get the feeling she was trying to *be* Hayley?

CHAPTER EIGHT

"Thanks, Caroline. I'll send the guys over as soon as I can. I know they'll be excited to get rollin' again."

Hayley made a few notes on the desk blotter and exhaled a sigh of relief. "Finally. My guys can get back on track."

It'd been a fairly quiet week and according to JoLynn no more threats had been made. Maybe contacting the sheriff had done the trick. Then again, she wondered how anyone else would know about her speaking to the sheriff. An official report hadn't been made and she hadn't heard any tongues waggin' around town. All she could do was shrug it off and be grateful for the respite from the enormous pile of bullshit that had been plaguing her and her business as of late.

"If only Dad were around. He'd know how to handle all of this. Hell, Rocky, he'd kick all of their asses and be done with it." Rocky tilted his head to the side and stood on his hind legs, placing his front paws on her lap the way he always did when he sensed she was in need of a friend.

Lately, she found herself thinking more and more about her absent father. If only he'd stayed longer, fought harder and been the kind of dad she'd needed. Even if he couldn't be the nine-to-five kind of dad most of her childhood friends had, he could've made more of an effort. Every daughter needed a father figure and for far too long, Hayley clung to the gaping hole in her heart where the spot for her dad's unconditional love had been.

She'd never been a naïve child. Many of her schoolmates had parents who'd gotten divorced and she knew from an early age that her parents were never going to be happy together. However, most of those kids had parents who'd worked shit out enough to be civil. Their dads came and got them every other weekend. Hayley would've given anything to have more time with hers. Being with her mother, Vivian, everyday had been less than conducive to being a happy child. Between her constant psychotic rantings and emotionally abusive outbursts, Hayley would've been better off being orphaned instead of being subjected to living with Vivian and the parade of drunken men she'd invite into and blatantly desecrate the only home Hayley had ever known. One of her favorite things to do was make a big dramatic shit show whether anyone was there to witness it or not.

"You'll never amount to shit! You're as bad as he is. Shit for brains. That's what you've got. Shit. For. Brains. Just like him."

"Yes, mom. I'll try to be better."

"Ha! Worthless. Don't look at me like that. It's like lookin' at his goddamned face every minute of every fuckin' day with you."

"Sorry, mom."

Day after day, it was insult after insult. The countless nights of sobbing into her pillows to muffle the worthless feeling that consumed her seemed endless. She looked forward to going to school each day just to get away from Vivian for a few hours at a time. Hayley dreaded snow days, holidays and summer vacations. All of which meant being stuck in that hellhole with her egg donor. When degrading her with hate-filled words no longer phased her only child the way the old bitch had expected and when the venomous verbal blows no longer hit their mark, she then began resorting to physical ones that left bruises where no one would be able to see them.

Shortly before one of her mother's long, drunken benders, Vivian gave Hayley the beating of her life; tossing her down a flight of stairs and kicking her as she tried effortlessly to get back up.

"Mama, stop! Please! You're hurting me!"

Another kick and some hair pulling had Hayley twisting and thrashing in agony, crying out until her voice was raw and emotionless. When the woman was finally exhausted by her efforts and could no longer deny the call of the raging alcoholic inside of her, she left. Broken and battered, Hayley lay there shocked into a painful silence unlike any she'd ever experienced before. Unable to move without hurting like hell, she slowly and painfully inched her way onto all fours, her hands covered in the clumps of hair that had been ripped from her head. From that night forward, all hope for a miracle to come and change her mother was lost. Gone was the last bit of naivety Hayley had inside of her. Hate took over—a hatred born of hurt and pain that would only be replaced by duty when her mother became too volatile to be anywhere except rehab.

When Vivian was in rehab, Hayley was able to relax and prepare for what her own future held. She went to school and had two jobs to fill her time. Her senior year of high school was one of preparation. She played the dutiful daughter, showing up for visitations with Vivian, both of them smiling and acting as though their love for each other was deep, unbreakable. Then, Hayley would leave the rehabilitation center and go straight to her weekend job. By the time she graduated, she had saved enough money to move far enough away from her mother and start a new albeit poor life. Gathering her from the rehab center and taking her home was the final step of her past life and the first of her new one.

Without a single tear shed, she spoke matter-of-factly. *"Welcome home and goodbye, Vivian. You'll never have another chance to hurt me. Enjoy your miserable existence alone. Forget you know me. Forget you ever even gave birth to me. I've already forgotten who and what you are."*

After depositing her mother in the front yard of their old family home, she pulled out of the driveway, never looking in the rearview mirror. The house that had been built by the loving hands of her great, great grandfather had also built the woman Hayley had eventually become. She vowed to be stronger than that nineteenth century monstrosity and with her she took pride in knowing she was a survivor. It wasn't easy. The past always had a way of creeping in, but for Hayley, it never consumed her—at least she didn't believe it did. One couldn't miss what they'd never had. Could they?

"Hello? Hayley?"

She'd been so lost in her memories she hadn't even heard JoLynn arrive.

"Hey there. What are you doin' here? It's your day off."

"Oh, I know. I was just in the neighborhood and thought I'd bring you a snack. I've been bakin' all mornin'. Coffee cake. Want some?"

Her friend stood in front of her desk, dressed in another outfit similar to the one she'd also chosen that day, but today her hair was different.

"What did you do to your hair? It's beautiful."

"Oh, I love the color of yours so much. I thought you wouldn't mind it if we looked like twins for a bit. It's just temporary. Tryin' it out to see if I like it or not." JoLynn tossed her head back in laughter. "Don't you just love it?"

Not in the least, but she would never dream of offending her. "Yeah, it's very nice."

Her tone must've been less enthusiastic than her employee expected, because she immediately piped up. "Like I said, it's only a temporary color. It'll wash out in a few weeks. But I thought it'd be fun to see if it will confuse the guys."

Yeah. Because my curvy body would easily be mistaken for your stick-thin and athletic one. "I think it's great. I'm sure the drivers will definitely be surprised when they see you."

"Speaking of drivers. Did Aiden tell you he took me home the other night? I totally forgot to mention it since we've just been so busy around here."

Oh, did he?

"Nope. I haven't really talked to him much this past week. He's been fairly busy himself."

JoLynn carried the coffee cake into the adjoining kitchen, calling over her shoulder, "Oh, I bet he has. He's such a sweetheart. Wanted to make sure I made it home okay after the incident with that package the other day. He was so worried about my safety. Bless his heart!" Placing her hand over her own heart, JoLynn's eyes took on a dreamy quality and her enormous, blindingly white smile told Hayley she'd also had her teeth bleached recently. The woman's enamel was practically glowing like the high beams on a semi. And if she wasn't mistaken, JoLynn's face had that slightly puffy, redness that happened when someone had just gotten Botox.

Yes, siree. Bless his heart and yours, you fake, plastic bitch. "Well, I'm glad he got you home safely."

"Oh, yeah. We had a few drinks and spent a long time talking. He's really super sweet. I'll never understand why you haven't snatched that hot hunk of man up. Seriously. Just thinkin' of him makes me wanna . . ."

"Okay, then. Too much info, JoLynn."

"Aww, sugar. I didn't know Aiden being with me would bother you. So very sorry."

The tone of her voice and the way she'd drawn out those last three words had Hayley seething with anger on the inside. She needed to dig deep and find her professionalism before she lost her shit on the leggy woman standing before her. What the actual fuck? Did she even have the right to be pissed or jealous? It was her own fault for not jumping on Aiden. She'd had her chance plenty of times.

Hayley grabbed a stack of papers, determined to focus on work. "No worries. Did you get that filing done yesterday?"

With a very noticeable eye roll, JoLynn placed her hand on her hip. "Of course I did. I'm not lazy."

It wasn't the first time Hayley had noticed the way JoLynn's accent came and went—sometimes seemingly at a will of its own.

"Well, with you seein' Aiden now, I have to be sure you're still doin' your job." Knowing the sickly-sweet smile on her face was enough to nauseate anyone, she continued, "I can't have someone droppin' the ball around here. Especially now that freight is ready for the guys over at Mason's."

"Oh? Are they ready to roll?"

"I'll find out for sure in a few. I was just about to call and let Mason know." Tucking a stray curl that had escaped her ponytail behind her ear, Hayley let out a sigh. "I just hope it's not too little too late."

"It'll be fine. Why must you worry so damn much all of the time?" Venom dripped from her bitch-dipped tongue and annoyance flashed in the woman's eyes.

Taken aback at the woman's tone, Hayley tilted her head to the side and pinned her employee with her best I'm-the-one-in-charge-here look. "Excuse me? Do we have some kind of problem here?"

JoLynn rubbed her palms down the front of her short denim skirt—a skirt very similar to the one she herself was wearing. "Sorry. Just having a bad day."

"Really? You seemed to be quite fine when you were trolling on and on about how great Aiden is. What's changed in the past few minutes?"

"Must be PMS," she said with a shrug.

"Yeah. Must be. Well, I need to get back to work. Please do the same."

Hayley waved her out of the inner office. Rubbing the back of her neck with her fingertips, she tried to will the impending migraine away. Sure she had her meds with her, but she hated giving into taking them. The doctor had offered her a daily preventative medicine, but she just wasn't fond of any prescriptions—let alone one she could possibly become dependent on. Hayley rarely drank. Yes, she'd had a few wild nights in her life, but after watching her mother, Vivian, consume copious amounts of wine or vodka mixed with orange juice to the point of being a raging alcoholic, she swore she'd never become like her. Coffee and dark chocolate were her go-tos when she needed a pick-me-up or an indulgence.

"Back to business. Mason's gonna need some time to get his guys in gear, Rocky." Dialing his number, she waited as the phone trilled in her ear. When the ringer switched to his voicemail, she realized she was a bit sad at only being able to hear his smooth, southern drawl in a short message. It finally hit her how much she missed hearing from all of her driver's this past few weeks.

"You've reached Raisin' Kaine Trucking. Leave a message. I'll call ya back as soon as I can."

"Hey, Mason. Hales here. You've got loads if y'all want 'em. Let me know as soon as you can so Caroline doesn't give 'em to anyone else. Give Savannah my love. Bye."

Talking to a machine had to be one of the least favorite parts of her job. So goddamn impersonal. Knowing she really shouldn't call Aiden until after she spoke to Mason, Hayley busied herself with other paperwork until Mason gave her an answer one way or another. Besides, calling Aiden wasn't something she wanted to do either. She feared the jealousy and irritation she was feeling would be palpable—even over the phone and she probably wouldn't be able to stop herself from bringing up his visit to JoLynn's place. Nope. She needed time to process and gather herself before having to deal with him.

"And just how am I ever going to be able to do that without making a complete ass of myself?" Mentally and emotionally exhausted, she leaned back in her ergonomic office chair and stared at the ceiling above her.

CHAPTER NINE

After he felt confident Hayley would be safe and JoLynn was at the office, Aiden turned his pickup around and headed towards home. He'd been tailing her for almost a week after the evening he'd followed her home. On the surface, JoLynn had everyone fooled into believing her to be helpful, kind and beautiful. However, everything Aiden had seen and heard thus far had him seeing her in a completely different light.

He'd sat in his pickup outside her house that night watching as she made a show of getting ready for bed. She'd pranced around the home, curtains wide open and giving Aiden much more than a glimpse of what was under the tight clothing she'd worm that day. His stomach churned as she paraded room to room wearing nothing more than a pink lacy bra and panties. JoLynn reminded him of the countless lot lizards he'd encountered across the country. All of them were willing to give themselves away to anyone who'd give them attention or money and she was no different. The way she behaved confirmed his initial beliefs of the woman—she was up to no good and she disgusted him. All he needed was the final report from Sheriff Baynes and he would go straight to Hales with irrefutable proof.

Among the many things that had the wheels of his mind spinning, was Mason. The silence between them had gone on long enough. He knew there'd be more tension soon because Aiden had agreed to haul a hot load up to Ohio. If things went well, he'd have the chance to get on a dedicated run and he'd no longer have to worry about fighting for freight. He could only hope that Mason would be mature about it and understand he had to look out for himself and his own livelihood—the same way anyone else would in the same position would.

Pulling into his driveway, Aiden parked close to the house and walked out to his ninety-nine canary yellow Pete. Climbing into the cab, he inserted the key and pressed the ignition button. When the five-and-a-quarter Cummins roared to life, he checked the many gauges on his dash to be sure everything was working and the truck and trailer were airing up properly. After a quick cursory glance at the interior of the rig, he made a mental note to remember he needed another pair of gloves for fueling up later.

Pushing the door open, he noticed a grease smudge on the interior tan leather just below the door handle. "Damn. How'd I miss that?" Making quick work of cleaning the spot, he gave the inside of the door a complete wipe down.

With that task finished, he climbed out of the Pete, closing the door before continuing his pre-trip inspection. A walk around both the truck and trailer checking tires, airbags, wagon straps, tarp and panels took him another ten minutes. Lifting the tail panel, he used the step on the back of the aluminum trailer to get into the MAC. In ninety-degree heat, the interior was a scorching one-fifteen and almost immediately, Aiden's grey sleeveless t-shirt was soaked in sweat. Another great aspect of being a trucker, he knew all too well how many shirts a guy could go through on a hot day.

Before every trip, drivers were supposed to do a thorough pre-trip check, but Mason had taught his guys to do more than that. Even though the truck hadn't budged in a few weeks, they all knew to take inventory of their coil racks, ratchet binders, chains, rubber mats, beveled six-by-six oak timbers to prevent the coil in place and large pieces of carpet or wool moving blankets they used in order to protect the coils that weren't wrapped in protective paper. Clients would reject any coil that was scratched, dented or warped in any way. When they did, the cost came out of the driver's pocket. Of course, there were drivers who just didn't give a fuck. Not Mason's guys.

For a forty-five-thousand-pound steel coil Aiden, Mason, Tex and Romeo had more than an adequate amount of equipment and always a stash of extras in the event they needed it. Straps could break, chains and binders could be stolen. Anything could happen out on the road. Like anywhere, people weren't always honest. Sadly, too many of them were up to no good and only looking to gain whatever they could for themselves. They'd either steal equipment for their own use or sell it out on the road.

With all of his equipment present and accounted for, Aiden lowered himself down out of the trailer, re-securing the tail panels and bungee straps. Aside from a quick shower and packing a small bag of snacks for the short trip, he was ready to roll. Back in the house, he stripped out of his clothes, leaving them in a tidy pile on the bathroom floor and climbed into the shower. When his phone began trilling with the loud ringtone he'd set for Mason, *Get in The Ring* by Guns 'n Roses, he was a bit shocked.

"Damn. You'll have to leave a message, bro."

Scrubbing the grimy dust and sweat from his body, Aiden allowed the luxury of hot water and being in his own shower as thoughts of sharing the large space with Hayley filled his head. With soapy hands, he reached down grabbing his slick, soap-coated and painfully hard cock. Pressing his free palm to the cool, wet tile of the shower wall, he pumped himself, imagining his friend's small, soft hands were doing the job.

He pictured her easing down onto her knees, looking up at him with those big eyes of hers filled with hunger and insatiable need. Her lips forming a perfect 'o' as he'd allow the hot water to rinse the soap from his body and dick. All the while his hand pumped faster and faster the closer he imagined Haley at eye level with his groin. Her lips would be warm, welcoming and slick as she made love to him with her mouth. In and out he'd glide—harder, deeper until neither of them could deny the need to have him inside of her.

Aiden would lift her with ease and she'd guide him into her core until his cock was nestled inside of her. The hot water would be no match for the heat emanating from their tangled bodies pressed against the shower wall. He'd fill her, sliding in and out of her as she rode him. His fingers digging into her ass while Hayley would use her own hands and fingers to explore his shoulders . . . his chest . . . his neck. The need to touch every inch of her, kiss every inch of her would rival his need for sweet release. He needed to claim her as his, mark her with loving nips all over her beautiful body and watch as passion blazed in her eyes.

Being her shy self, she'd have a momentary second of embarrassment when she'd realize he could see every deliciously naked bit of her in the bright bathroom—her tanned skin a direct contrast to the stark, sterile room. With one kiss, he'd make her forget—make her embrace the moment with her legs wrapped around his waist and she'd forget everything except the way they felt about each other. Pumping and milking himself, Aiden could almost feel her walls tighten around him, clenching his dick until neither could take no more and their bodies would pulse with complete satisfaction as his hot, creamy load was washed down the drain and he came back to his lonely, cold reality.

The harsh, incessant ringing that let him know a voicemail was waiting for him echoed in the plain, white tiled bathroom while Aiden dried off and dressed in work clothes as his fantasy pulsed on in his mind. Sliding the phone into the back pocket of his jeans, he carried his dirty clothes to the laundry room, Aiden hung up the t-shirt and lay the jeans flat on top of the washer so that they'd dry while he was gone. Placing the soiled clothes in the hamper would be disgusting and lazy—two things he wasn't.

Annoyed by the incessant ringing of the phone, Aiden grabbed the phone out of his pocket, hit the appropriate icon and listened to the message.

"Hey, man. Hayley called."

Aiden's heart clenched just hearing her name being spoken. "Man, you've got to get your head on straight or just man the fuck up and go tell her how ya feel." Talking to himself was pointless. Aiden already knew what needed to be done.

"I'm assuming she's got loads for us. I'll let ya know what I find out after I call her back. Just wanted to touch base with ya. Later."

With a sigh, "Great." It wasn't that he was unhappy about freight coming through, but Aiden knew this day would come. He and Mason needed to mend fences anyways. It was time, but it'd have to wait until after he got back from Ohio.

Tossing a few drinks and food items into a small cooler, Aiden grabbed his wallet and keys before leaving the house, locking the door behind him. Feeling slightly guilty that he had to get on the road and the other guys were still waiting for something to come through, Aiden climbed up into his rig, buckled up and headed out of town.

The CB, like always, was full of chatter and annoying noise from the truckers he passed out on the highway.

"Where's my chicken at?"

"Ya got yer' panties on?"

"Fuckin' smart cars are the dumbest fuckin' things in the world."

"Fuck you. I like smart cars, asshole."

"Nah, fuck you, pussy. What kind of driver likes a fuckin' smart car?"

"Who's got my panties?"

Aiden grabbed his mic. "Oh, for fuck's sake. Really? What the hell is wrong with y'all?" Listening to the morons out on the road could drive a person mad if they let it and a man could only take so much. "Grow the fuck up and keep the channel clear for important shit."

"Fuck you, man! What are ya? The cocksucking CB police? I'm out here all day every day and I'll talk about whatever the fuck I wanna talk about. Got it?" The man hollered across the airwaves.

Aiden knew it was pointless to respond, so he did his best to tune the assholes out, instead listening for reports of state troopers or traffic situations as he drove onward towards Florence, Kentucky where he'd grab his coil. He'd never understand how some of those assholes had women waiting for them at home. Who the hell would want to be chained to any of those foulmouthed and crazy fuckers? He'd wager they were all small-dicked and treated their women like dogs. The respectable ones were far and few between. Lately, more of the crazy came across the airwaves than the sane did.

"Hey, Phoenix. Ya listenin'?"

'Tanker', a well-known hauler for Gibson Fuel came through Aiden's speakers loud and clear. "Yeah, man. What's up?"

"Where ya headed?"

"To Florence and then on up to Bowling Green in Ohio. How 'bout you?"

"Man, I'm headin' south. It's about to get crazy as fuck northbound."

"Why's that?"

"Where've ya been? The presidential candidates are comin' to Cincy and with 'em, are a shitload of protestors."

"Fuck." Aiden knew he needed to guard his words carefully. He wasn't one to start shit involving politics or social climate. In fact, he never, ever got involved in anything pertaining to current events while he was out on the road. "Dude, I haven't been out here for a few weeks. Are these the same protestors I just saw on the news?"

"Yeah."

"Protestors! Protestors!" Some mindless jacknut horribly sang and the shrill pierce to his voice gave Aiden an instant headache.

"Hey, Tanker? Thanks for the warning. I'll avoid the main leg and head out on the other side to avoid the chaos."

"Good idea.

"Travel safe, man. See ya 'round."

"Ten-four and you too."

The country seemed to be unraveling at its very seams. Was there anything that could be done to break down the barriers, pain and anger that had erupted into a full blown frenzy of rage and fear? In all of his thirty years, Aiden had never seen such division and discord in America. The blatant disregard for human life, the denial of rights for not just some, but for everyone and the all-out lack of common decency was enough to make one lose hope for all humanity.

The riots reminded him of the news reports from years earlier that he'd heard about while he was out on the road a month ago. A man had been pulled out of his semi and beaten to death after the killing of a man in California. People were angry then and they were angry now. Aiden knew it was human nature to stand up for what someone believed to be either right or wrong, but recently, protestors were again attacking trucks.

Hundreds of people were shutting down major interstates and highways in protest. Though illegal, to an extent, the police could do nothing about it unless someone was hurt or if their lives were in danger.

Last week, they'd pinned in a tow truck driver—a man who was just trying to do his job. The man wasn't unsympathetic to their cause, their pain. Yet, the protestors surrounded him, chanting *"Fuck that truck!"* and *"Get out coward!"* at a deafening volume. What had the trucker done to them? Nothing. The same could be said for the men, women and children basically being held hostage in their own vehicles out on the freeways. Like anyone else, they had jobs and families to get home to. Why would the protestors put so many lives at risk?

To Aiden, it didn't make any sense to go to that extreme. Most of the people he knew out on the road just wanted to deliver the good they were hauling and make it back home alive. They just wanted to do their jobs. That meant delivering any and everything humans use, eat, want and need. The last thing he wanted was to be put in an even more dangerous situation. Hell, life on the road was a risk every second of the day.

Why can't people understand that?

Where were the people who should be outraged at the seventeen million empty and abandoned houses that should've been given to the seven-million-plus homeless military veterans for serving their country? Where were the people who should be helping to put an end to the shitty mental and physical care that those very same veterans received? How about the fact that too many veterans were not receiving any care and at least twenty-two, maybe more per day were killing themselves? Why weren't more people pissed and doing something to put an end to that? Women and children were being trafficked and sold into sex slavery rings. Many of them taken right to the center hub out in Missouri and shipped by truck to or from Mexico. But did anyone in power give a rat's ass? No. They'd rather keep everyone riled up, pissed off and hating each other instead of doing something to stop the suffering on every street, in every neighborhood in every town.

If all of those protestors would join hands with everyone who was suffering in America, so many things could be fixed—so many people could be helped. Instead, it seemed as though more and more people would rather see the destruction of society than help another in a truly peaceful and meaningful way. And that was heartbreaking to Aiden. Why did it feel as though compassion and integrity were becoming a foreign notion?

Hell, maybe he spent too much time thinking. Out on the road, he had little time for anything else and he'd seen plenty in his years of being in the high speed rodeo. Most of it, he wished he could unsee and if any of it were an indication of what was to come in the future, America and maybe the world was in a shitload of trouble.

CHAPTER TEN

"Hey, Hales?" JoLynn's nasally twang was becoming as hard to deal with as potato bugs were in July. When had she gone from feeling protective of the woman to experiencing instant irritation?

"Yeah?"

"I'm gonna head out early if ya don't mind. I've got to take care of somethin' back home."

"Back home? Like at your house?"

"Nah. Back in Paducah. Mama called and my uncle is real sick. I gotta head that way."

"Can't your mama take care of things? You do have a job here, ya know."

Irritation was clearly visible upon JoLynn's face, but she continued. "Ya know, it's drier than a popcorn fart as far as freight is concerned. My uncle is sick." She popped her hip to the side, planting her palm on it. "I asked nicely. I do all of the menial shit you ask me to do like I'm some kind of damn grunt worker and I don't ask for much. So, the least you could do is be a bit fuckin' understandin' about a family emergency."

Whoa. What-the-ever-living-fuck? "Well, I didn't know you were so unhappy here, JoLynn. You knew what the job entailed when you begged me to hire you. If you're not happy here, please feel free to move on. Now."

JoLynn spun on her heels and she huffed aloud as her heels clacked across the hardwood floors. "God, you're such a bitch and a jealous one too. No wonder Aiden chose me."

Bitch.

"Bless your delusional heart, JoLynn. My dear," she called, "there isn't one thing about you that I'm jealous of. Now I don't know what's gotten into you, but whatever it is, you can take it and your high maintenance ass back to whatever holler in Paducah you crawled out of."

All Hayley could hear were drawers slamming and stuff being tossed into what sounded like a cardboard box. The occasional mumble erupted from the fray happening in the other room, but she chose to ignore it. She had bigger things to worry about than her soon-to-be ex-employee's temper tantrum. If she were honest with herself, it was both a relief she'd be gone and yet, a bit of an inconvenience. That so-called grunt work JoLynn did everyday was work she just couldn't always handle on her own anymore. With freight picking back up, it might get dicey.

"Oh well. I built this business and I'll be damned if I don't keep it runnin' myself." She blurted, silently cursing herself for saying anything about it—even to her own empty office.

With one last evil glare, JoLynn strutted in and came to a stop in front of Hayley's desk, box in hand and hair askew. "Hope you're happy now. I broke two nails. I'll send you the bill."

Hayley couldn't suppress the laughter that bubbled out of her. "Oh, you send it. I'll be sure to file it just the way you would, sweetie. Now, run along."

She wiggled her fingers at the angry and flustered woman. JoLynn squinted her eyes and with flaring nostrils, she pinched her lips together, clearly wanting to say more. But when Hayley sat there smiling at her, the anger JoLynn was exuding gave her immense joy at the sight of the other woman's normally well-polished appearance now in shambles.

The woman could flaunt her supposed one night with Aiden all she wanted, but after some thought and reflection on the matter, deep down, Hayley knew she wasn't the kind of woman Aiden would ever settle down with. If someone were to look at the entire package JoLynn truly was, they'd realize one thing to be true of her. She was no better than a typical lot lizard from the hills who'd used anyone she could in order to pay for her lopsided thirty-six-double-dee-rack, a ten cent dye job, extensions that had seen much better days and some fancy clothes. Assuming she'd get ahead by pretending to be something she clearly wasn't, JoLynn went about it the wrong way and the façade could only last so long. Hayley surmised that once people caught onto her shenanigans and saw JoLynn's true colors, they got as far away from her as quickly as they could.

After the angry woman tore out of the driveway in cloud of dust, spraying gravel against the side of her office building, the events of the past ten minutes sank in. They'd gone from being friends and having a business relationship to a full-blown nuclear meltdown in a proverbial blink. Hayley wasn't the kind of person to intentionally hurt anyone, but once her buttons were pushed, watch out.

"What the hell just happened?" Rocky perked up, raising his head with ears standing at attention.

Grabbing her cell phone, she called Aiden. "Just in case I'm mistaken about Aiden and his choice in women, he needs to know what he's getting into with that one." Tapping her fingers on the desk as she waited for him to answer. "Don't give me that look, Rocky. I wouldn't be a true friend if I didn't warn him. Any . . ." her voiced cut off as she listened to Aiden's new voicemail greeting.

"Hey, friend. I really need to talk to you. Give me a call as soon as you get a minute."

No sooner did she hang up, her phone rang. Without looking at the screen to see who it was, she swiped the phone icon to answer. "Hey there. That was fast."

"Hi, Hales. Sorry I didn't get back to you sooner. What's up?"

With a sigh, "Hey, Mason. I wanted to let y'all know those state fair rides came through and I need to know if y'all can get started tomorrow afternoon?"

"Hell yeah. That's great news? Where's the first jump?"

"You'll be headin' to Oklahoma and then on to Texas from there. Are ya sure ya wanna do this?"

"Works for me. Of course we're takin' these loads. Why wouldn't we? How many trucks ya need?"

"Well, with Savannah being so close to delivering, I wasn't sure you'd be able to go. To be honest, I need every driver you can get."

"Sav and I've already talked about this. She understands. Ronnie is already here to help out, but I was hopin' she'd deliver the baby before the loads came through. Here we are. Still waitin'. Stubborn kid already." Though he laughed, pride and anxiety were clearly detectable in his voice.

"Sure seems like that little one is pretty content in her belly. I guess you're not gonna tell us if it's a boy or a girl until that baby arrives, huh?"

"Not my choice." He chuckled. "Sav is determined to keep it a surprise. And whatever she wants, she gets."

Hayley couldn't suppress a giggle. Her friends were so in love and so very blessed. She couldn't wait to see the three of them together once the baby arrived. "Well, I better be one of the first people y'all tell."

"You know it. Besides, I'm sure Sav wants you and Ronnie at the hospital when the time comes. I guess just keep your schedule as clear as you can in the coming days."

"Will do. Before I forget, I need to give you Caroline's phone number. She'll be the first person you'll deal with on these loads. Once you talk to her, she'll give you the outfit owner's info." She recited the woman's number and information from a file she'd created on her computer.

"Thanks, Hales. Is there anything else?"

She knew she shouldn't, but when had that ever stopped her. "Mason? Are you and Aiden gonna be able to do this?"

A short silence on the other end of the line told her he too had concerns. "It'll be fine. I haven't spoken to him yet, but I tried callin' him earlier. We're currently in a game of phone tag. Not sure where he is."

With a sigh of relief, she smiled. "Great. I'm playing the same game. Glad y'all will get things worked out."

"You bet. Life's too short, right?"

"Yep. Well, I'll let ya go. I'll call Caroline and let her know everything is set on my end and you can get in touch with her when you can. Call the guys and have 'em ready to roll. Give Savannah hugs from me."

"You got it. Later, Hayley."

"Bye."

The minutes ticked by painfully slow as she anxiously waited for Aiden to return her call. "Maybe he's pissed at me? What if JoLynn already has her French manicured claws in him?"

She needed to stop. Thinking about all of that bullshit was goin' to drive her insane. There wasn't anything she could do until he got back with her. Hayley busied herself with calling Caroline and checking other load boards, emails and text messages, gathering load information for her other drivers. She didn't have a large operation, but for the time being, it was sufficient.

"Maybe I'll be able to expand after things pick back up."

But did she truly want to? Sure, knowing the guys now had loads was great, but if she were honest with herself, she didn't even have a life. Perhaps it was time to find another agent for the guys and move on.

"Move on to what though?"

Her entire life was built around the business. Her home was here. Aiden was here. Even if they weren't together and could never be, she was still able to see him and talk to him. Then again, she thought, with JoLynn in the picture, that'd probably change too.

Too wrapped up in mindless nothings, the sharp ring of her phone startled her back to reality.

"Aiden." She blurted as soon as she answered.

"Hey, darlin'. What's happenin'?"

Man, that voice! Goosebumps rose on her arms, sending a shiver through her body. "Are you free tonight? I was wondering if you'd like to grab a bite out at Joni's?"

"Well, I'll pull in around midnight. Is that too late?"

She hated to wait that long, but what choice did she have? It wasn't like she could tell him everything over the phone. "Oh, you're out and about right now? Well, midnight works for me. I'll meet ya there."

"I took a hot load to Ohio. Sorry I didn't wait like the other guys, but I was goin' nuts sittin' still. Is there anything else ya needed? Don't get me wrong, I love hearing your voice. But, you don't sound right, babe."

Tears built up from the frustration of the past weeks filled her eyes and she barely swallowed the lump in her throat. "Just a long day. Y'all have carnival loads starting tomorrow. I'll tell ya all about it tonight when I see ya. Okay?"

"Ten-four. See ya then."

"Travel safe, Aiden."

"Always. Guess I'd better call Mason too. See if I can get ahold of him this time. Bye, darlin'."

****

When Hayley arrived, Joni's was still bustling at the late hour. After all, truckers were out and about on the road twenty-four-seven. Every table and booth was full, but she knew Aiden was already there waiting. His text was a short one, but made her stomach flip with the excitement of seeing him.

"I'm here, darlin'."

From clear across the crowded room, she could see his green eyes, twinkling. Saying they called to her would be such a cheesy and corny thing, but to her, Aiden's eyes . . . all of him, was the closest thing to home she could imagine. What she wouldn't give to see those eyes alight with pure carnal pleasure.

She smiled, making her way to his table and he stood to pull her into his embrace. "Hey there, stranger." She gave his cheek a quick peck and slid onto the cushioned seat of the booth.

"I haven't heard from you either, sweetheart."

"True. I know you've been busy with . . . stuff." Hayley spun and fidgeted with the tight napkin-rolled silverware in front of her.

"Hales," he reached across the table, taking her hand in his. "Ya know I'm never too busy for you. Call me day or night."

Her breath hitched at his touch and before she could stop herself, she blurted out the words she never thought she'd say. "What about JoLynn? Won't she mind? I know about your night together."

A look of confusion crossed over his face. "Our night? Together?"

"She told me all about it."

"She did, did she? Well, guess what, babe." Amusement and a hint of something she couldn't quite figure out lit his eyes. "She lied. I never spent a night with her. I was spying on her. Baynes and I knew she was no good and I'm just waiting to hear from him about the rest."

"Why? What's going on?"

"It's a long story. We can talk about it after we eat. But know this, nothing and no one is going to get past me to hurt you. I guarantee it. That woman is crazy and you need to stay as far away from her as you can. I suggest getting rid of her."

What in the world would make Aiden and the sheriff spy on JoLynn? Up until the past week, she had known JoLynn was a bit weird, but there wasn't anything to be fearful of when it came to the woman. What was she missing? All she knew was that Aiden was protecting her from some unknown threat and that meant the world to her.

"JoLynn isn't the kind of woman I'd ever want. You must know that, darlin'. She isn't you."

When those words left Aiden's lips, the game suddenly changed and Haley could feel a big change stirring within her. Wings, the same ones she'd believed had been clipped by the harsh realities of her life and that one stupid rule, were beginning to flutter. She was about to take the biggest leap of her life. She was going to fly as hard and as fast as they'd carry her into the arms of the delectable and dangerous man who sat across from her. It was time for her to stop being afraid. It was time to live—even if it were only for one night with the man she'd sworn she'd never date—the same man she'd tried to convince herself that she didn't love.

But she hadn't said she'd never fuck him senseless, had she?

CHAPTER ELEVEN

"Hales? Are you okay? Say somethin', sweetheart."

"She isn't me? You weren't with her? Why would she lie like that?"

Aiden couldn't explain what her breathy voice and glassy eyes were doing to his body. All he knew was that it took every ounce of control he had to not kiss her full, pink lips that trembled when she spoke.

"No, darlin' and to be quite honest, I truly think you need to get JoLynn out of your life as soon as humanly possible. She's bad news."

"She's already gone. I fired her today."

"Wait. What?"

"Why do you dislike her?"

"I just don't trust her. Not after everything I saw when I was following her around. She hangs out with some shady lookin' company."

Man, he really didn't want to be the bearer of bad news. However, even without the official report from Sheriff Baynes, the way JoLynn had been behaving and now, finding out that she'd lied about him to Hayley really pissed him off. No sooner had he opened his mouth to fill her in on everything he'd observed, his phone rang.

"I've gotta take this, babe. I'll be right back." Sliding out of the booth, Aiden unfolded himself and walked out of the restaurant as he answered the call. "Hey, Baynes. What did ya find out?"

"We were right. The woman is trouble. I'm not sure what she's after, but she isn't who she says she is."

"Really?"

"The only thing real about her is her first name. The scrap of paper from that package that I snuck out of Haley's office had enough of a fingerprint for us to get a hit. She isn't from where she said she is and her rap sheet is pretty extensive. Nothing major, mind ya. Domestic disturbances, drunk and disorderly. She has a penchant for being obnoxiously loud and abrasive after closing down bars. There's an arrest on record from a few years ago when she passed out in the hallway of some ritzy hotel during some kind of convention that was being held there. Looks like she was one of the workin' girls, if ya know what I mean. Apparently, she became violent and defensive when she was asked to leave."

Aiden's anger and concern were mounting. *What kind of fucked up individual sent threats like that to someone they liked and worked with? And why?* With a deep breath, he tried to maintain a calm façade as the conversation continued.

"She sounds like a real piece of work." Aiden opened the doors and stepped out into the night. The smell of diesel fumes was thick and heavy on that side of the trucker diner, but the cool, midnight breeze felt good against his face.

"Yeah. She's from deep in the holler and her mama had her arrested a few times when she was younger. Looks like mom and daughter are one in the same. Trash."

"Why is she out to get our girl? Can anything be done to put her away? With the amount of threats she's thrown towards Hayley, there's obviously room for more than simple concern here. She could be in real and immediate danger."

"I'm heading over to speak with her in the morning. I'll give her a chance to tell the truth. While I'm doing that, you can ask Hayley if she wants to press any charges against her."

"You got it. I'll tell her right away and if I know her like I think I do, she'll be more than happy to press charges. Thanks, Sheriff."

"You bet. Nothin's gonna happen to our girl. Not with us lookin' out for her."

"True."

"Aiden? Keep an eye on her until we get this all sorted out. Ya never know what kind of crazy is just waitin' to happen inside the head of a woman like JoLynn."

"Believe me, I know. JoLynn even tried to convince Hayley that I spent the night with her. She's already made another move, so I'm working on clearing that up right now."

"Good Lord. All right, keep me posted and I'll do the same. Have a good night."

"You too."

Aiden slid the red icon on his phone, ending the call and took a deep breath before heading back inside. There was no way he was letting Hayley out of his sight until this woman was caught and locked up where she needed to be. With Hayley on her shit list for some reason, they couldn't just sit back and pretend that everything was okay.

"Everything all right?" Hayley asked as he sat back down across from her in the booth.

"It will be. Sheriff had some news." Reaching across the table, he held her hand. Those soft fingertips and the way her hand fit in his made his heart race. He'd protect her from the world if she'd let him. "Let's talk about it later, okay?"

"But, Aiden? I'd rather we left. I'm not really hungry anymore. Not for food."

That glimmer in her eye! Was that what he thought it was? Could she truly be...

"What?"

She tugged his hand. "Let's get outta here."

A bit confused, but he wasn't stupid. If she wanted to be alone with him, alone they'd be. He threw a couple bucks on the table for the waitress as a way to thank her for letting them take up her booth space and hand-in-hand, he walked Hayley outside. They'd barely reached his semi when she spun, pressing her palms to his chest, turning him and backing him up against the grill of the Pete.

In an instant, she stood on tiptoe to kiss him. Gentle at first, then more insistent. She stood on her tiptoes, wrapping her arms around his neck, pulling him closer to her and kissing him deeply. He explored every inch of her feminine lines, lifting her off of her feet as she circled her legs about his waist. Her mouth tasted like the vanilla gloss she wore and her hair, her skin smelled of fresh spring flowers. With every kiss, every breath, he fell deeper into her and Aiden knew he was gone. The beautiful woman in his arms would be his end or his salvation. For one moment, one night with her, he knew it was worth the risk of finding out which one it'd be. But not in that parking lot. Not like this.

"Darlin'," coming up for air, he caressed her cheeks. Her skin warm and rosy, eyes dark with desire and need—just the way he'd always pictured her when and if she'd ever be in his arms this way. Looking deep into her eyes, "I don't know what's gotten into you and I want you more than anything I've ever wanted in my life, but we can't do this. Not here. You deserve more than a tumble in my truck."

When she worried her bottom lip, it nearly undid him. The confining fabric of his jeans was no match for the erection spurred by Hayley being in his arms with her heat pressing into him. "Does it really matter? I want you." Leaning in, she nibbled at his ear lobe. "I want you now, Aiden." She whispered.

Dear God, he must be a saint or really fucking stupid! "Hales?" He tipped his head back, enjoying the moment of pure ecstasy as she trailed tiny, hot kisses along the side of his neck. "I want our first time together . . . to . . . be . . ."

"What? Special?" She giggled. Reaching between their bodies, she used her fingers to follow the outline of his cock which was molded by the coarse fabric of his jeans. "I don't think this can wait for special."

Fuck!

He was gonna shoot a load right then and there.

No.

He couldn't allow that to happen. "Babe, as much as it pains me to say this, we need to either get to your house or mine. I plan on making you scream from more pleasure than you've ever known. That . . . can't . . . happen . . . here." He panted through clenched teeth.

"I'd say it's about to. Whether you like it or not."

Damn it. In one fluid motion he scooped her off of his waist and flung her over his shoulder. "Again, I don't know what's gotten into you but I like it. What took ya so long?" Opening his door, he climbed the step and sat her down on the passenger seat of his truck. "Now, you're gonna sit there and behave until we get to your place. Hear me?"

She leaned back, pressing herself into the seat and with one slender finger began tracing the lines of her lips before dipping it inside the very hot, very wet mouth he'd just been kissing. "You've got a bed right there." She hooked her thumb toward the back of his rig.

"Shit." He wouldn't cheapen this moment. She deserved better. Hayley was a lady and he was gonna give that lady the ride of her life as soon as they were behind four walls and as far away from other people as they could get.

Shutting the passenger door of the cab, he willed himself to think of and whisper the dumbest shit he possibly could in an effort to calm down. There was no way he could safely get them home with a raging boner threatening to jump out of his pants. The hard-on ached, needing to be released from its denim and cotton prison as he walked the entire length of the truck and trailer before making his way up the other side to his own door of the rig.

"Bunnies. Bunk. Big bunk. Lots of room. Damn. Dogs. Puppies. Kittens. Bubble Gum. Lips. Hayley's lips. Kisses. Flowers. Hayley's skin. Fuck. Fucking Hales. No. Making love to her. Sonofabitch, this isn't working."

He'd just have to drive like a bat out of Hell because the only thing he could think of was their two naked bodies entangled, every inch of her sun-kissed skin pressed against his.

Climbing into his side of the truck, he turned the key and pressed the ignition button, the diesel engine roaring to life. He wouldn't, no he couldn't look directly at the seductive temptress sitting beside him. Out of the corner of his eye, he could see her—long legs crossed, twirling a stray strand of dark hair around her fingers, a lick of her lips and Aiden almost lost his mind.

Fuck it. Without waiting for the truck to be fully aired up, he released the brakes and shifted the Pete into gear.

"Aiden?"

"Nope. You stay quiet. The sound of your voice is gonna send me over the damn edge."

Her giggle sent lightning bolts of need rocketing through his body. "I mean it, babe. I'm drivin' way too fast and all I'm thinkin' about are the things your mouth could be doin' right now."

"Sorry, but I thought you should know that we should really go to your house. It's closer."

With a quick glance in the side mirror, he changed lanes and headed out of town.

"Besides,"

"Hales." The deep growl coming from his throat shocked him.

She paused when he pinned her with a look and then, she laughed like the sultry little siren she was. "I can't wait to get you out of those clothes, Aiden. The sooner, the better."

She was trying to get them both killed. Plain and simple.

CHAPTER TWELVE

Like a stallion racing across wild, barren terrain, Aiden drove with unerring abandon toward their destination. Anticipation and excitement at finally being beneath him, at last feeling his touch on her most intimate places, was almost too much to bear. Why had she waited so long? Her heart and body were meant for his. The moment their lips touched, she knew this to be true. Why had she denied herself the one true pleasure in life that everyone should have the chance to experience? Why had she allowed her entire life to be controlled by what had happened in her past? No more. This man sitting across from her, earnestly trying to hide his painful need as he ushered them across miles of highway, was her future.

Any man who cared enough to treat her as though she were a virgin being bedded by her first love after years of tolerating a platonic relationship and yet, was capable of ravishing her with his eyes was the man for her. He was complex, multi-faceted and mentally, she already knew him intimately. Being with him wouldn't be bad luck and her life wouldn't turn out like her mother's had. She was stronger. . . so much stronger than Vivian had ever been.

So maybe she hadn't been wrong to wait. Maybe this was exactly how her life was supposed to go. Having that final, beckoning, lightbulb moment might be one of those things that'd been written in the stars. It all sounded so cheesy, so corny to her as the thoughts raced through her mind and her body hummed with longing to have Aiden inside of her. Cheesy be damned! She was ready for this . . . ready for whatever being with Aiden brought her way.

Aiden pulled into his long driveway and parked quickly. Without waiting for him to have the Pete shut off or locked up, she bailed from the rig and he followed on her heels. In a flash, they were in each other's arms as he fumbled to get the key into the locked back door of his house and they practically tumbled inside, using his boot to kick the heavy door shut behind them. Neither tearing their eyes away as they kissed, stumbled through the darkened home in a frenzy of busy hands and buttons flying off of shirts. The tiny bits of pearl and metal hitting the floor couldn't be heard over their heavy breathing and soft moans.

Their awkward tongue tango combined with trying to undress each other reminded her of a fumbling mess meant for a blooper reel on one of her favorite TV shows and Hayley quickly found herself giggling.

"Fuck this." His words came out as a growl, spurring her need into overdrive as Aiden scooped her into his arms and carried her to the bedroom.

"Too many clothes." Her own voice sounded foreign to her. Who was this vixen that was amped to tackle him like a linebacker and ride him as if he were a derby thoroughbred?

Her head swam and tunnel vision took over with one mission in mind. Ripping the shirt off his chest, she ran her hands over every well-defined inch of the man's skin and muscles while he removed the rest of his clothing. Taking a step back, she admired the body of the man standing before her. The moonlight shining against his backside and casting a larger than life shadow across his pale hardwood floors. Without a thought, she told him to do what she'd always wanted to say to him.

"Turn around, Aiden. Face the window."

Hot damn! Hayley always knew that ass was going to be all she'd imagined it to be and boy, was it ever! Stepping closer, she allowed her fingertips to trail along his neck, shoulders, down his arms. With the lightest touch, she began again. This time, starting at the top of his back and following his spine slowly, inch-by-glorious-inch until she reached the arch in his back right above that masterpiece of muscle. Cupping his ass cheeks, she gave them a squeeze as she lovingly trailed kisses across his skin. His body tensed when her lips touched him and she blew warm air over the places she'd kissed him.

"Hales." His voice no more than a hoarse whisper, sent shivers through her body.

She moved in front of him and slowly peeled the shirt off of her shoulders. He reached for her and she waggled a finger at him.

"You made me wait. Now, it's your turn."

"But . . ."

She silenced him by removing her jeans and panties, followed by a quick flick of her wrist. The front closure on her lacy bra opened easily, revealing to him her barely covered breasts bathed in the moonlit glow of the room. With the lightest touch of her fingers, the scrap of lace fell to the floor along with the rest of the clothing at their feet. Without another word, they embraced each other.

"I've wanted you for so long." He murmured, the rough stubble on his chin scraping her hot skin as he tasted her lips and neck.

"Yes." One word. The only coherent word she could make herself say. Her mind was a wreck, her body begged for more of him.

His tongue was like oxygen fueling the flames within her. Moving them closer to the bed, Aiden placed one palm at the base of her back, holding her close with the other as he masterfully lowered them both to his bed. Surrounded by down and a thick, cotton duvet, Hayley felt like they were making love on a cloud.

Reaching for him, she stroked his cock. Touching the tip with one finger, she found what she desired. Bringing the damp finger to her lips, she licked the tip, eliciting a small moan from Aiden as he watched her every move. She needed more. His scent, his taste—uniquely his, were all-consuming.

Lowering his mouth to her breasts, he took a rosy bud into his mouth. She arched upward, reveling in the pleasure and pain as he playfully bit at first one and then the other. Hayley ran her fingers through his hair, tugging and pulling, pushing his mouth against her body. Feeling the scrape of his teeth against her skin and his hot, wet tongue as he used it to trace circles around her nipples wasn't enough. He was toying with her. Two could play at this game.

With a gentle nudge, she pressed his shoulder back, forcing him to lay flat on the thick bedspread. Straddling his middle, she pressed her wet, hot mound against his hard cock but didn't take him inside of her. Aiden grabbed her hips when she began to roll them and his eyes rolled back in his head.

"Woman, you're killin' me."

She fondled and played with her breasts as she sat above him, giving him a show. With each movement, she felt his dick swell beneath her. When she was sure she had his full attention, Hayley leaned forward and dangled her tight, rosy nipples above his face. Taunting him with a chance to suck on them, she crawled backwards down the length of his lean, hard body until her breasts covered his cock and the tip of his dick was almost touching her chin when she looked down between their bodies.

With a quick lick of her lips, Hayley squeezed her breasts together, moving her body forward and back, pumping his dick between the soft skin of her firm globes. Embracing her inner porn star, she watched as Aiden moved beneath her, she felt another rush—one of control and dominance over his pleasure. It was ecstasy in itself knowing she had him exactly where she wanted him . . . in more ways than one. Far from done, Hayley flicked her tongue out, licking the tip of his cock each time she pumped him. When she could take no more of the teasing that she herself was also experiencing, Hayley released him from her breasts and took the full length of him into her mouth, deep into her throat.

With a gasp and a gritty growl, Aiden held her head between his large hands as she sucked his cock. Raising his hips off of the bed, each thrust going deeper between her lips. Soft moans and unintelligible words came from him as she sucked faster, deeper and then to a slow, long, tight gripping suck that had him arching his back and letting go of her head to press his palms against the sturdy headboard. When his forceful pressure caused the wood to make a loud cracking sound, she released him from her mouth and in one fluid movement, he rolled her onto her back.

Leaning forward, he opened the drawer of his nightstand and withdrew a condom from inside. Hayley took it from his hands and tossed it to the floor.

"We don't need that. I've got it covered. Just make love to me."

"Babe, I want to make sure your protected. I'm not taking advantage of you."

Barely suppressing her laughter, she said; "I appreciate how thoughtful you're trying to be, but I'll be fine. Been on the pill for years now. I want to feel you, all of you. And I think we're both on the same page. If anyone's taking advantage of anybody, it's me. Or have you forgotten how we got here in the first place?"

He couldn't argue with her logic, so without another word, he slipped first one and then another finger into her slick folds, stroking her walls until he found that hot little button that sent her into the orgasmic stratosphere.

She felt as though her own skin would melt away from the scorching heat emanating between them. "Yes! Oh . . . God . . . More!" If ecstasy were a sound, it'd be the way her lust-filled words reverberated around the stark room, coming back to her as she begged and begged for more of him. All of him.

Before she came back down, he placed the tip of his cock just inside her, slowly inching himself in until he could go no further. Hayley lifted her hips, wrapping her legs around his waist and pulled him closer as he thrust into her. The feel of his thick cock sliding deep and pulling back just enough to make her bring him back with the force of her legs was mind-blowing as she climbed to a climactic plain unlike nay she'd ever felt before.

First a small quiver within her, then a steady pulsing as he pumped and she milked him as he caught up with her. Hayley thrust her head back, chin pointing toward the ceiling as Aiden filled her with everything he had, coating her, claiming her. He collapsed atop her and as they lay there panting, caressing, exploring each other, Hayley knew she'd never again be the same woman she'd been before she'd kissed him that night. Everything would be different from now on.

CHAPTER THIRTEEN

Please don't let it have been another fantasy.

The weight on his body causing him to stir, Aiden opened his eyes to find his dream come true draped across his chest.

Dear God, she's beautiful.

Careful not to wake her, he planted a soft kiss on her forehead and wrapped her in his arms. Holding her was the best thing Aiden had done in decades. The stillness of the house, Hayley softly breathing as she slept and their hearts beating in unison was almost as perfect as the night before had been. In all of his life, no other woman he'd bedded—there hadn't been that many, maybe a handful, had ever given him so much pleasure. A simple touch of her hand gave him a high that all of those years of gambling and having piles of money could never come close to. After so many years of never having what he'd always needed, in her arms, Aiden was finally home.

He'd never been one to believe in happily-ever-after because there was never a reason to. Had he hoped?

Sure, but like everything else in his life, hope came and went. Now, as he lay there holding the woman who made him want to be a better man, he couldn't help but wonder if it'd last. Would he screw it up like he'd screwed up everything else? Hayley was the one person in the world who knew the real him and what if that wasn't enough for her?

He'd change. Aiden would be whatever and whoever she wanted him to be if it came down to that. When she woke up, they'd talk about what happened between them and once he filled her in on the whole JoLynn situation, they could move forward. She needed to know that she was in danger . . . real danger.

When she began to stir, he softly rubbed her shoulder and she nuzzled closer to him.

"Good mornin', handsome."

"Mornin', darlin'. How'd ya sleep?"

"Satisfied."

He chuckled. "Same here, babe. Are you hungry?"

"Honestly? Yeah, but I don't want to move from this spot. I'm kinda comfy here."

So was he. If it were up to him, he'd never leave the bed again as long as she was laying in his arms. "We've got a big day ahead of us. Well, I do."

Groaning, "I forgot. All of you are heading out on the road today."

"Yeah. Thanks to you." Bringing her hand to his lips, he kissed her fingers. "These hands of your yours are very talented. You work them to the bone for all of us and you worked my…"

"So you're saying I'm good at what I do?" She laughed.

"Darlin', you're amazing."

After a brief silence, "Aiden? Why didn't we do this sooner?"

He wasn't sure what to say. He'd been in love with her for so long, Aiden would've waited an eternity for her. "I'd say the timing was never right before now. Are you okay with this?"

"I'm more than okay. But, I'm kinda sad about it, to be honest."

"Sad? Why?" *Here it comes.*

"Because I didn't show you how I truly feel before now. I was too scared—afraid Vivian was right.

This can't be bad luck for us, right? I feel like a lot of time we could've spent together has been wasted and it's my fault. I've always known how you feel about me and now that I know you weren't with JoLynn, I've realized you've spent all of these years waiting and hoping I'd feel the same."

"No. Don't you even go there. My time with you was never wasted. I've loved being in your life in any way I could be. Even if you never felt the same, I'd still love you, Hayley. That won't change."

She rolled over, propping herself up on her elbows beside him. Hayley's eyes wide and shining, she worried her bottom lip for a bit before speaking. "Thank you."

"For what, darlin'?"

"For waiting. Somehow you knew the truth that I was denying to myself. Believe me, I've battled with my feelings for years. I wanted you. I wanted to be with you, but I was so scared, Aiden. You know how it was for me."

He knew. Vivian had been just as bad, if not worse, than his own birth parents had been. He brushed a tear off of her cheek with the pad of his thumb and smiled. "Darlin', I know and I need you to know it'll never be like that for us. I promise. If this is what you truly want, I'll always put us first. You'll never be lonely and you'll never feel alone."

"I want this more than anything. I love you, Aiden."

He gathered her in his arms, kissing her with the hopes that he was always kissing away any fears or doubts she might still have. To ease her mind and heart, he'd give anything.

"I love you more, darlin'."

She broke the embrace, slightly pulling away. "I'm such a sap when I'm with you." She shook her head, dark auburn waves tussling about her bare shoulders.

"Is that a bad thing?" He chuckled.

"Not necessarily. Don't you find me weak and unattractive when I'm like this?"

"Never. You don't always have to be so strong. If you need to lean on me or cry, that's okay. You're allowed to feel, Hales."

She nodded and he pulled her back into his arms. "That woman really fucked with your head, didn't she? My poor, sweet angel. Women like your mother should never have kids. I wish I could take away all of the pain you suffered at by her hands and mouth. No one deserves to be treated like you were. You're safe with me. Your heart will always be safe with me, darlin'. I swear."

He'd known about her childhood and growing up with Vivian, but until that moment, he hadn't realized just how much it had messed with her. Seeing her breakdown simply because she'd done something for herself and taken a huge leap by opening herself up to him by being as vulnerable as a person could be, broke his heart. No one should ever be made to feel as Hayley had. He'd make damn sure that it never happened again and if he ever came face-to-face with her mother, Aiden would let her know exactly what he thought of the despicable excuse for a mother she truly was.

After Haley's body grew less tense and more relaxed in his arms, he still held her tightly. "Now, I say we get up and have some breakfast. We have all the time in the world to catch up on lovin' each other. Right?"

She nodded, her tear soaked cheeks against his shoulder.

"Okay. So no more regrets or givin' our time to people and things in our past that have brought us to this moment. Agreed?"

"Agreed." Her breath was so warm and soft against his skin. "You're right."

"I know," he said, breaking the heavy feeling that had been in the room.

"Oh, here we go," she laughed, playfully swatting at him. "Enjoy that one, Mr. Hunt. Don't you know that the woman is always right? This was your only pass."

Aiden began tickling her under her ribs. "Oh, really? I bet I can get you to say it again—many, many more times. Trust me, darlin'. I'm good at what I do, too."

"Stop, oh stop, Aiden! It's . . . too . . . much! If you make me piss myself, I'll never forgive you." Her laughter filled the room and if his heart could smile, it would have.

"Okay, okay. I'll stop. For now, but you've been warned. I have my ways of makin' you succumb to my will."

"You're too much. Now, get that fine ass up out of this bed before I prove to you just how much of your will I can break."

With that, they both erupted into another round of laughter. "Seriously. We're not very good at being serious, are we? Those words sounded ridiculous coming from my lips."

Aiden watched as she eased herself off of him, stretching before climbing out of bed. Her curves were so beautiful. He'd enjoy tasting every inch of her again and again.

"Your words might not be serious, darlin', but that body of yours is no joke. I'm gonna enjoy doin' so many things with you—to you."

"Promise?" She flashed him that cock-hardening smile he'd fallen in love with years before.

"You can bet on it and some of those things are still illegal in other states." With a wink, "Like I said, you've been warned."

"Tease!" She walked into the restroom and he climbed out of bed, grabbing a fresh set of boxer briefs out of his dresser to slide on.

"I'll meet you in the kitchen, babe."

"Be right there," she called from the other room.

Being a man who needed coffee to function in the same way his Pete needed diesel to run, Aiden went straight to the coffee maker and got to work measuring out enough to make a pot of his custom ordered special blend. On the road, he didn't have the luxury of drinking great coffee. When he was home, he didn't settle for anything less than the Sumatra, Columbian and Ethiopian blend he bought from his favorite roasting company. Soon, the entire kitchen was filled the aroma he loved.

When he finished blending cream into his own mug, he filled and added Hayley's favorite powdered creamer to hers. It wasn't the first time she'd had coffee at his house. In fact, he kept an adequate supply of many of her favorite things so she had them when she visited. Years of being friends had taught him her various likes and dislikes which, strangely enough, they agreed on almost everything. She hated spaghetti and couldn't stand the way the tomato sauce infiltrated the ricotta cheese in lasagna. She said it was disgusting to look at and he had to agree. Beyond that, they both loved their coffee—almost too much some people might say.

"Cooooofffffeeee." He almost choked on the sip he'd been taking when she stumbled into the kitchen, growling in her impersonation of a zombie.

"Here ya go. Enjoy, darlin'."

"Oh, I will."

He loved the expression on her face whenever she drank coffee. Now, it reminded him of the way she'd been lost in ecstasy the night before and watching her sip at the hot beverage was making his dick hard all over again.

"Don't you wish there was a way to just get the caffeine directly into our brains? We wouldn't have to wait on it to cool down." He laughed.

"Nah. I need the caress of that hot, bitterness on my tongue. It must be swallowed." She winked at him over the rim of her pink and purple coffee mug—the one she'd insisted he keep at his house.

"Swallowed, huh? Are we still talkin' about coffee?"

"I think you know we're not, cowboy. But before we have ourselves another mattress rodeo, I'm gonna need food and so are you. We need to practice all of those illegal sexual activities. I plan on wearin' you out."

CHAPTER FOURTEEN

Breakfast ended up being nothing more than a few microwaved breakfast burritos and copious amounts of coffee before they raced back to the bedroom for another round of lovemaking.

"I'm so glad we opted for something simple. It was killin' me to keep my hands off of you for so long."

"Babe, you can put your hands on me whenever you want."

"Not today, though. You've gotta get movin'." Hayley tilted her head towards the clock.

"Shit. I sure do. Wanna shower with me?"

"You'll never get outta the house if I go in there with you." She wrapped her arms around his neck as he leaned down to kiss her.

"I love this."

"Kissing?"

"Kissing you. Only you."

"I'm kinda fond of it myself, handsome."

"Hearin' those words come from those beautiful lips of yours sounds so damn good."

Hayley knew she was blushing, but she didn't care. Being with him, loving him and allowing herself this wonderful, new experience was everything she'd always dreamed of. Nothing had gone wrong. Neither of them had regretted their shared evening. She was going to be fine . . . safe with Aiden.

"Well, at least come into the bathroom with me while I get ready. Before I leave, I really need to tell ya all about JoLynn before I head out on the road this afternoon." Taking her by the hand, he led the way.

The tone of his voice when he mentioned JoLynn let her know that whatever he was about to tell her wasn't going to be good. Combined with the clear urgency to make sure she knew before he left made it all feel even more disconcerting. What had she missed? The woman barely weighed a hundred pounds. It wasn't like Hayley couldn't handle herself if JoLynn decided to try anything crazy.

"Here's the deal."

Aiden turned on the shower knobs and the three strategically mounted shower heads began to fill the bathroom with steam within seconds. Hayley found herself feeling envious of the way the hot water was touching him in his most intimate places. Now that she'd felt his touch . . . his body against hers, Hayley wanted more.

"JoLynn isn't who she said she is. She's never lived in Paducah and she has a rap sheet longer than my MAC trailer. The woman is a lying piece of shit."

"Really?"

"Yeah, babe. That's not all."

She waited as he rinsed the soap from his hair—that gorgeous, dark blonde shade now a bit darker in the shower. She longed to run her hands through it again—just enough to mess it all up. Who was she kidding? It took every ounce of control she could muster just to sit in that same room and not rush into the shower and pin him against the wall. She was suddenly a sex fiend. Well, not suddenly. She'd finally found the man she was meant to be with and loved the way he satisfied her.

Clearing her throat, she asked, "What else could there possibly be?"

"Now, we don't know why . . . yet, but she's the person who's been behind all of the threats. Phone calls. Texts. Even the disgusting package."

What the fuck? There was no damn way!

Outrage and disbelief tangled for space inside her mind. "What are you talkin' about, Aiden? She was there almost every single time one of those things happened. She can't be the one behind it all. Furthermore, why would she do that?"

"Honestly, I don't know. Sheriff Baynes doesn't know either, but he's heading over to her place today to speak with her about all of it. He's got enough of a fingerprint on the package to press charges if you want him to. It's all in your hands, darlin'."

Hayley couldn't find the words to express the thoughts running through her mind. None of it made any sense at all. "What could she possibly gain by threatening me?"

Aiden wrapped a white, fluffy towel around his waist and stepped out of the shower. "No idea. She did her best to make you jealous of her supposedly bein' with me. That didn't work. But, I know there's more to this than it being about me. She didn't use that tactic until after the other threats had been made."

"And none of that makes any sense either. She had to have known I'd ask you about it—ask if it were true."

She watched as Aiden toweled himself off. "Or, she thought you'd be so upset and that you'd never speak to me again. Either way, she doesn't know either of us very well. Hell, I know she only saw me spying on her the one time and that was the night I followed her home after you left."

"Aside from the shady guys you saw her speaking with after that, is there anything else I need to know?" She paced back and forth across the white tiled floor, chewing on her thumbnail—a nervous habit that reared its ugly head when she was feeling overly stressed.

Aiden's furrowed brow let her know it was an answer she probably wasn't going to like. "I saw her naked."

"What? Are you fuckin' kiddin' me?"

He threw his hands up in surrender as she spun on him. "Half-naked. Really. Half. And I didn't enjoy it one bit. She's nasty and way too skinny for my liking."

"Oh, that helps a whole fuckin' lot, Aiden. Seriously. What the actual fuck?"

"Darlin', I was in my truck and across the street. I sat there waiting to see if she left again or if anyone else dropped by to see her. Ya gotta understand that I was very suspicious of her behavior and I was only there to find out if my suspicions were right. Nothing more."

Hayley knew she had no right to be so angry that he'd seen JoLynn's naked or half-naked bits. They hadn't been together. It was none of her concern. But damn it all, she wanted to rip out every bleach blonde stringy extension from the woman's narcissistic head and then feed it to her.

Trying her best to keep all of her rage inside and not unleash it on Aiden, she questioned, "What else is there?"

"Let's just clear up what I saw. Okay?" Aiden took a deep breath and continued. "She knew I was out there. I watched her purposely strip away bits of clothing and strut around that house, opening all of the curtains and acting like a slutty fool. It was sickening. Part of me thought I was overreacting by thinking the show was for me, but no one else showed up at her house. Around one in the morning, she finally gave up and that was after two hours of me sittin' in the truck. I don't know if she thought I'd just break down her door to be with her, but she couldn't have been more out of her mind and fuckin' crazy. I waited until she shut all of her lights off and I left shortly after. That's all. The rest of the week, I simply tailed her. Not once did she slip up other than chatting with some guys at a warehouse down on Summit Street. For a few days now, I was thinkin' I had it all wrong. Sure, she's a tramp and acts like a lot lizard in her own home, but who was I to judge? I don't want her. Never did."

"So, you're sayin' the woman taunted you on purpose. Thank you for not fallin' for her strip tease. But, why the hell didn't you tell about what was goin' on sooner? I'm not an idiot. I spent so many days with the woman that I kinda knew she was a bit weird. That doesn't excuse all of these secrets behind my back. Sure, we weren't together, but we've always been friends and friends don't keep things from each other."

"You're right. I messed up. I was just tryin' to protect you." He reached for her and she shrugged him off.

"Don't. Not yet. You've just told me that the three people closest to me in this world have been lying and going behind my back. Did you expect a kiss and all would be well? Especially after I opened myself up to you like I have?"

"To be honest, I guess I sorta did. Sorry, but I figured you'd be happy that Baynes and I were lookin' out for ya. I didn't realize I needed your permission before doin' that?"

Hayley felt her eyes bug out as soon as those words left his mouth. Whenever some guy at the office cocked off to her, the same thing happened. Big eyes and seein' red.

CHAPTER FIFTEEN

Holy fuck! What was I thinking? Did I really just say that?

Aiden knew he was fucked as soon as the words left his lips. Hayley stood in front of him, arms crossed and her eyes were so full of rage . . . no, hurt. Maybe both. Not even twenty-four hours and he'd already fucked up. Shit.

"Before you say anything, I'm sorry. I didn't mean to say that."

"But you were thinkin' it."

"I apologize for that too." He folded his hands. "Look, I'm not very good at this sort of thing. You already know I'm just a simple man who runs his mouth before he speaks. I'm sorry I hurt your feelings. I know you don't understand why we kept it all quiet, but we had to. I couldn't come to you before I knew everything. I didn't want to worry you if there was no reason for worry."

"That's my call to make, Aiden. I'm not a poor, defenseless woman in need of some Peterbilt drivin' knight in shining armor. Nor am I some nitwit."

Aiden knew she was more than capable of handling herself and therein lay part of the problem. She'd have taken matters into her own hands instead of allowing the sheriff to handle things the right way. The legal way. Besides, the last thing Aiden wanted was to be refereeing some hair-pulling cat fight.

"Look, darlin'. I can stand here all day in my towel arguin' with ya, but I'm not sorry that I was doin' what I thought was right. I knew Baynes was investigatin' her and the threats. If I'd have told ya, you'd have gone in there half-cocked and ready to rumble with that skank. That couldn't happen. Obviously there's more to this situation than any of us knows about. So, you can either put your pride aside and accept that I meant no harm to your precious independent woman sensibilities or whatever and that I did this out of love for you. Or ya can spend the rest of the day bein' pissed off at me for somethin' I can't and wouldn't change. I've gotta get ready to hit the road. The choice is yours."

Her eyes were narrow slits and he braced himself for the torpedo of backlash he figured he'd be facing. Even at her angriest, he just wanted to wrap his arms around Hayley and hold her until she was no longer upset. Dealing with women was one of the things he'd never master. Then again, how many men could say they had? To him, tearing a five-fifty engine out of his Pete, rebuilding it and putting it back in would be easier than figuring out how women think. Often he wondered if they felt men were just as difficult to figure out.

"Look," she pinned him with a glare. "Believe it or not, I do understand why y'all did what ya did. That doesn't mean I can't be a little bit," raising her hand, she pinched her thumb and forefinger together until they were almost touching, "upset about the way it was handled. That being said, I shouldn't have unleashed my anger on you. Thinking about the way JoLynn made a direct threat at Rocky, a tiny dog who has nothin' to do with whatever fucked up and twisted ideas she's got in that empty head of hers, is unforgivable. Luckily, I won't have to deal with her any longer and yes, I will press charges against her. I'll tell the sheriff myself."

The calmness of her tone left Aiden feeling confused. Where were the hysterics, the throwing of things?

"And another thing. My precious independent woman sensibilities are tellin' me to get to work. I'll talk to you later. Safe travels and call me if you have any problems."

He watched as she strode from the room and began gathering her things. "Hales, don't leave like this. Come on."

"Aiden," she fastened her jeans and slipped her shirt over her head. "I'm just goin' home to get ready for my day. There's nothin' left to be said right now. I'm not throwing a fit. I'm not even angry. I just need some space."

"All right, then. Take my pickup. I'll come get it after we get back from this first jump next week or so." When a woman needed space, a man had better give it to her. That's the only thing he truly knew about the opposite sex. "Call me later? Or should I call you?"

"Thanks." She grabbed his keys off the counter and walked the length of the house with him following behind. Aiden opened the back door for her and when she looked up at him with tears in her eyes, he felt like he'd been kicked in the gut.

"Darlin'?" Aiden's phone began to trill. "It's Mason."

"Take the call. We'll talk later. Bye, Aiden."

Damn. "Hey, man. What's goin' on?" Not that he cared. All he could think about was Hayley walking away from him as he spoke.

"Well, we're havin' the baby! I'm takin' Sav to the hospital right now. Woooooo!"

The baby.

"That's great, man. Try not to scare herself with your drivin'." He chuckled.

"Shut up. Here's the deal. I need you and Tex to get the truck fueled up for me. I didn't have a chance to get it done. Sav went into labor last night and fuelin' up was my last priority. Can ya do that for me?"

"Sure. But, are you really leavin' out as soon as she has the baby?"

"Do I want to? No. But, for now, this is how it has to be."

"And she's all right with that? Man, she's gonna kick your ass when you get back."

"Honestly, she won't. I've never known a woman as strong as she is. Ronnie's with us, so she'll be right by her side when I can't be."

Aiden watched as Hayley tore out of his driveway in a cloud of dust and gravel. He happened to know a pretty strong woman too. Only he hadn't given her the benefit of the doubt and he hadn't been man enough to stop her from leaving.

You just let her leave. Idiot.

"That's good. All right, then. I'll get ahold of Tex and have him get started. I'll meet him there in a while."

"Thanks, man. We're having a baby!" Mason's hollered and cheered before hanging up.

"Lucky bastard." Aiden smiled to himself. Mason had it all and Aiden wasn't afraid to admit that he was pretty fucking jealous of him.

Pressing the speed dial button for Tex on his cell phone, he waited patiently as the tone rang on the other end.

"Hey, Phoenix. How ya doin' man?"

"Good for now, Tex. Mason just called. Savannah's having the baby, so he needs us to go fill up the trucks and have 'em ready to roll."

"Isn't it great? Ronnie just called to tell me they're on their way to the hospital. She said Mason is drivin' that pickup like he stole it! Ha! Man, oh, man. Can't picture him as a dad, can you?"

"Not really. But he is." The men shared another laugh over picturing Mason changing diapers.

"Dude, he gets grossed out at truck stops. How in the hell is he gonna handle baby shit?" Aiden exclaimed.

"This is gonna get real interestin'. Hope Savannah takes lots of pics of him or video . . . video of him on diaper duty would be fucking hilarious!"

After they were done amusing themselves, their conversation returned to the matter at hand.

"I'll get started with Mason's truck and after ya get here, we can tackle the rest. Romeo is supposed to meet us in Texas. Not that I was thrilled to be headin' down there to begin with, but now, we'll have to deal with that fucker."

"We'll talk about all that later, bud. I'll be there as soon as I can."

"Ten-four."

Romeo was on the run, too. Shit. Things are gonna get real interesting.

Hanging up, Aiden immediately called Hayley's phone. When it went straight to voicemail, he left her a short message.

"Hey, darlin'. I know ya' need your space, but I thought you should know that Savannah's havin' the baby. They're on their way to Memorial right now. I'm headin' over to help Tex get the trucks ready. If ya need anything just call. I'll be here." A brief pause as he was about to hang up. "I love you. No pressure. Just wanted you to hear it again."

Knowing it'd take a while for Tex to get to Mason's house, Aiden cleaned up the remnants of his and Hayley's breakfast before moving onto the bedroom to strip the bed. Only after getting irritated again and again that the towel around his waist kept slipping, did he realize he hadn't dressed yet. Absent-mindedly, Aiden combed through his still damp hair, put deodorant on and then threw on the usual; briefs, well-worn jeans, socks, boots and a black t-shirt before cleaning up the rest of the house. He refused to leave a mess sit all week while he was on the road. Plus, it helped him think and fool himself into focusing on other things instead of on Hayley.

Who do ya think you're kiddin'? She's all you're gonna think about until you hear from her again.

He couldn't argue with himself on that one. Her scent was everywhere—present, yet fading. So, when he stumbled upon the pink, ponytail holder she'd left behind, he brought it to his nose, inhaling the sweet smell of the conditioner she used and loved. Knowing it seemed like a creepy thing to be doing—sniffing the fabric like some sort of lovesick weirdo, he placed it on the bathroom counter.

"God, don't let me have fucked this up. I need her."

CHAPTER SIXTEEN

"Shit. Shit. Shit."

Hayley rested her elbow on the inside of the pickup's door as she drove away with tears blurring her vision. Pressing her free hand to the side of her neck, she felt the telltale signs of another migraine trying to rear its ugly head.

How in the world had a wonderful evening and morning with Aiden taken such a disastrous turn?

Because you let your self-righteous bitch out to play. That's how.

She hadn't even meant to. Between all of the stress, secrets and the flippant way Aiden had spoken to her, she'd reached her limit. There was only so much a woman—even the strongest woman, could take.

For fuck's sake. You treated him like shit. He's your best friend and now, your lover. If he doesn't just hit the road and never look back. Great job, Hayley. Maybe Vivian was right about you after all. Shit. For. Brains.

Maybe she shouldn't have been so bitchy, but he should've known he could trust her. Was she supposed to swallow her pride and jump right back into bed with him after all the lies and secrets? Hell no. A line had been crossed. Many lines, in fact. She might not have much, but she'd be damned if she'd toss her pride to the wind.

How satisfying has your pride been so far? Has it kept you warm at night? Has it given you multiple orgasms? I didn't think so. Pony the fuck up and act like a mature adult. Fix this with Aiden. He's leaving and anything can happen when they're out on the road. You know that.

No matter what she told herself, her heart was hurting and the sting of Aiden's revelations would take a little while to get past. With that thought, her phone rang. "Speak of the devil." She sent the call straight to her voicemail. "Not now. Just not now."

As she drove through town and out past Horsefly Valley, the curvy roads reminded her of a wild snake. With no edge or center lines, Hayley carefully maneuvered the jacked-up, lifted truck around the curves and over the hills until she reached her own place back in the woods near Farmer's Retreat. She'd have to have someone from Joni's bring her truck back to her place later. She couldn't leave it sit there for a week until Aiden returned home.

Once she'd parked the gigantic Ford in her driveway, she practically ran from the truck to get to the sanctuary she called home. Inside, Rocky awaited her.

"Hello there, handsome." She ruffled his fur behind his ears, holding him tight against her chest. "Thank you for being such a good boy."

With a quick survey of the house, she could see he'd used the potty pads she'd put down for him the night before. Nothing was torn up and he'd barely touched his food.

"Want a treat, little dude?" She reached for the package of beef jerky strips he'd do anything for.

"Are you a pretty boy?"

Without missing a beat, Rocky sat on his hind legs, raising his front paws and tilted his head to the side as he flashed what she always called his smile. No one would ever convince her that it wasn't. He was a happy guy and she was grateful every day that Savannah had convinced her to bring him home. Aiden was just as smitten with him as she was. Which was a great thing. He'd never really seemed like the small dog type and that had worried her at first. Weeks ago, after their first movie night spent with Rocky laying across both their laps on the couch in the living room, they fit together like a family.

Family and she'd treated him like crap that morning. "Why does it have to be so hard?"

Grabbing her phone, she resigned herself to listen to the message from Aiden.

"Oh my gosh! Savannah's having the baby!" She danced around as Rocky stared at her with bewilderment before he joined in, chasing her around the kitchen. Obviously the word 'baby' and dancing referred to him . . . in his mind.

"Damn. Now that JoLynn is gone, I can't get to the hospital until I'm finished at the office."

She spent a few more moments visiting Rocky and cleaning up the soiled potty pads by flushing what could be flushed and placing the wet absorbent paper thin squares into her trash bin.

"I'll take that out before I leave. Let's get you outside for a quick walk and then, it's time for me to get showered. There's a baby comin' and I'm not gonna miss it."

After walking the small dog and then showering with what felt like lightning speed, she grabbed the first pair of panties and one of her bras out of her antique dresser. It was piece she'd found at a local yard sale and refurbished herself. It wasn't perfect, but she loved it and it served a purpose. Closing the drawers, she snagged a pair of jeans off of a hanger and a yellow V-neck sleeveless top. It hadn't always been her favorite color. The purchase of it had been one of function other than fashion. Now, it reminded her of a comforting, breezy Kentucky Summer and that always made her smile.

Aiden's last words from his voicemail earlier were etched into her mind. Allowing herself the time to get away from the situation, unwind and grab some alone time had done wonders for her state of mind. She made up her mind to call him back once she got to the office and made sure everything was still set in stone for Mason's guys for the week.

"The office. Shit. Rocky, you'll have to be a good boy a little while longer. I can't take you with me today. I'll be back as soon as I can."

She applied her makeup, combed through her waist length hair and pulled it up into a ponytail. Once that was finished she retraced her steps to the kitchen, chose a few potty pads and hurried back to the bathroom to place them on the floor beside his replenished water and full food dish. With one last special treat for Rocky, she gave him a kiss before heading toward the door.

"Love you and be a good boy."

When he gave her a quick tilt of his head, she blew him another kiss before leaving the house.

Being early enough in the day, she avoided the rush hour and tourist traffic with ease. The gravel and dirt road that led the way to her office seemed a bit different as she drove Aiden's truck up the skinny lane. She had to admit it was a nice ride, it just wasn't something she'd choose for herself. If she weren't in a hurry, she'd have grabbed the small step stool to assist her with climbing back up inside. When she'd left Aiden earlier, the adrenaline pumping through her veins fooled her into charging at the mammoth of a truck at full speed. Being on the shorter side, it proved to be more difficult than she'd expected. She was glad he hadn't offered to come out and witness her embarrassing attempts at getting behind the wheel. With her luck, Aiden would've offered to help her onto the driver's seat using any means necessary. Knowing him, it would have been awkward or another chance for him to toss her over his shoulder to get her up in there. In theory, it sounded romantic. In reality, it smashed her boobs and hurt a bit riding on his hard, chiseled shoulders.

"That would've just made my damn day."

She laughed as she pictured the way Aiden would've helped her by lifting and shoving on her ass as she pawed at the leather seats with sweaty hands, slipping and sliding until they'd both would've given up, collapsing against each other in a fit of laughter and make-up kisses. In fact, that would've made her day. That's how her day should've gone. Instead, she'd 'flown off her goose' as Savannah's friend, Ronnie, liked to say when anyone was clearly out of their mind.

Pulling to a stop in front of the office, it occurred to her that she practically lived there. "Might as well move into the damn place."

Hayley acknowledged she worked a lot, but today with her friend having her very first baby, she should be there to support her and Mason. Sometimes, she felt like she had entirely too much of her life tied up in work. On one hand, it saddened her and on the other, she was just grateful to have something of her own. With so much on her mind and all of the crazy stuff that had happened as of late, maybe Savannah had been right. Perhaps she should take a vacation while Aiden was out on the road with the guys. Their loads would be handled by the fair manager and his agents. In fact, the other guys she loaded could be loaded from anywhere. Why not take her laptop, phone, Rocky and hit the road?

With all of the places and possibilities for an adventure running through her mind, she let herself into her office and tossed her keys onto her desk. Heading straight to her coffee maker, she made quick work of brewing a pot of her favorite blend. Once there was enough in the pot for her to slide the glass carafe out and place her mug under the filter basket, she allowed the stream of hot liquid to fill her mug. Replacing the carafe just as quickly, Hayley added creamer and took a long luxurious sip of the rich and dark roast. Between the burst of caffeine and future plans, her mind and body were buzzing with excitement.

The hand that snaked out from behind her caught her off guard, sending the cup of hot coffee flying across the room as she grappled with the fingers closing over her mouth.

"Welcome to work, bitch."

CHAPTER SEVENTEEN

Rolling down the interstate, black smoke flying out of the seven-inch chrome stacks of his, Aiden clicked the button on his Bluetooth, answering his phone in the hopes it'd be Hayley.

"Hey there?"

"Phoenix? Is that you?"

The feminine voice on the other end of the line sounded familiar but he couldn't place it.

"Yeah, who's this?"

"Memphis. And Phoenix, you really need to get out here to Triple F. They've cornered Tex?"

"What? Who?"

"Some guys. I don't know their names, but they're beating the ever-livin' hell out of him. Please hurry!"

Shifting gears, Aiden mashed the accelerator and started weaving through traffic, passing cars on the left and right.

"Memphis, call the cops. I'll get there as soon as I can. I'm about ten minutes out. I'll probably still get there before the cops. Call 'em anyways. Hear me?"

"Got it. Just hurry. They're messin' him up bad and I couldn't get ahold of Mason. Tex needs backup in a major way and no one here will help him!"

"Sit tight. I'm on my way."

What the fuck is going on?

Aiden pushed the icon that allowed him to voice dial. "Hayley." The phone and Bluetooth connected immediately and he flew through the traffic like a NASCAR Camping World Truck Series professional as he waited for her to answer. When the ringing finally switched over to her mailbox, he hung up. Obviously she was busy or maybe still irritated with him.

With no choice but to fill her in later, he ended the call and concentrated on getting there as fast he humanly could. Luckily, the exit ramp for Triple F, Food, Fuel and Family Plaza, was a short two miles away. Aiden hadn't begun his day expecting to kick some ass, but he would fuck up whoever was attacking his friend. It must be pretty bad for Memphis, the fuel desk clerk, to have called him. She was a quiet woman, single mom and quite pretty. If those assholes even thought about touching her, he couldn't be held responsible for what happened to them at his hands.

Easing onto the exit ramp, Aiden took the right lane and made another right into the plaza parking lot. Spotting Mason's truck parked at an angle on the exit side of the fuel island, he barreled through the lot, coming to a screeching halt, blocking the entrance side with his own rig. Three men had Tex cornered against Mason's Pete and Memphis stood at the outer edge, anger lighting her face. From a distance he couldn't make out what was in her hand, but it appeared to be small.

"What the hell is she doing?" Aiden flung open the driver's door and ran right into the fray.

When he got close enough, he could see that Memphis was in fact holding a very small twenty-two—the kind a woman could carry in her purse and grab quickly if the need arose.

"What the fuck's goin' on?"

Before Aiden received an answer he raised his fist, smashing into one of the men's jaws and knocking him out with a hard uppercut.

"Fuck you, Phoenix!"

"Wanna tag team a guy when he's all alone? Suck my fuckin' dick asswipe!" Aiden blocked the second guy's attempt at kicking him and spun him around, giving Aiden the right angle to wrap his arm around the guy's neck.

"Listen, mother fucker. I don't know who ya are or what ya want and I don't fuckin' care. I've had a really bad day and you've fucked with my friend. That means your day is more fucked up than mine. You're one buddy down, another is bein' held at gunpoint. I suggest you kick fuckin' rocks."

"Fuck you. Ya think I'm scare of a washed up piece of shit like you, Phoenix?" The man's gargled words came out in a spray of spittle across Aiden's arm.

Aiden tightened his grip on the man when he tried to struggle. "Do ya hear me? I've got nothin' to lose and time to fuckin' kill. You're nothin' but a detail on my to-do list today, fuckhead."

The man, Aiden now realized looked familiar, tried to stomp on Aiden's foot and kick him in the shin.

"Really? That's the best ya got, boy? Come on, man." Aiden flung him away with a shove and laughed as the guy landed on his ass.

"You're gonna regret that, dick." The man wiped sweat and spit off of his face with the short sleeve of his dingy white t-shirt and stood up, squaring his shoulders. "Your friend here thought he was all that, too. I'd say he learned his lesson. You're turn."

The man charged at Aiden and before he could get within three feet of Aiden, the guy tripped over his own feet, face-planting on the asphalt parking lot. Aiden left the whimpering, bleeding man laying where he fell.

"Yeah. Ya sure showed me, hero."

Aiden spun his attention to Memphis, the other man and Tex who had slunk to the ground. He could see lesions on his friend's face and blood dripping from his forehead. He needed help and soon.

"Memphis, ya got that yahoo over there?"

"Sure do, Hun. He ain't nothin'. This is the nutless one of the group. If he makes any sudden moves, I'll be sure to make that a reality for him."

Aiden watched as the man's face drained of color and he raised his hands high above his head.

"Alrighty then."

Leaning down to assess his friend, "Man, you're a goddamn mess. Can ya stand up?"

Tex groaned in reply. "Hold tight, man. Help's on the way."

He didn't want to move him, just in case he was worse off than he looked. "Memphis, why don't you lower that and sit with Tex until help arrives."

"You sure?"

"Yeah."

"By the way, where the hell is Romeo? Shouldn't he be here too?"

"Don't ask me. That guy is his own mess. Sit down beside him just in case he slumps over. We don't need him bashing his head on the ground."

After the long-legged beauty, hurried to Tex's side, Aiden focused on the last man standing, slamming him against the side of Mason's truck with a hard shove and pinning him there with his forearm under the guy's chin. If he pressed any harder, the guy's trachea would collapse. It took every ounce of control for Aiden to ease off. "Who the fuck are y'all? What the fuck do ya want?"

Even before the guy could get enough air into his lungs to speak, Aiden knew who they were.

Fuckin' JoLynn's scurveball friends. What the fuck?

The man at his mercy must've noticed the realization dawn on Aiden's face. "You already know who we are, don't ya? Yeah, that's right. Kick all our asses, loser. But guess what. We've got you right where we want you and your precious lady friend is all alone." He tried to laugh and only managed to choke as Aiden reapplied hard pressure to his throat. "Or is she?" He squawked.

Hayley! In one fluid motion, Aiden released the man and as he bent over to gasp for air, Aiden caught him with a hard right hook, sending him to the pavement where his cronies lay.

Mother fuckers! "Memphis, I hear sirens. Can you stay here and deal with them? Hayley's in danger and I've gotta get to her."

He was already backing away towards his rig when she called, "Go ahead. I can handle it from here. I'll keep ya posted."

With a nod, he jumped into the driver's seat, released the parking brakes and started grabbing gears before he'd even shut his door.

Sonofabitch! It was all a fuckin' trap! Hold on, darlin' I'm comin.

Aiden flew towards Hayley's office, calling her on the phone with no luck of her answering and he called Sheriff Baynes.

"I heard there was trouble. But now, it's involvin' our girl? How far out are ya?"

"I'll be there in five." Navigating the backroads like he was driving a sports car, Aiden cut across the outskirts of town, speeding over the hills and only slowing the rig when he came to sharp curves.

"You'll beat me there. My guys are out at Triple F right now. I'll get to ya as soon as I can."

They hung up their phones at the same time and Aiden spent the next few minutes praying he wasn't too late.

CHAPTER EIGHTEEN

"Whiny, jealous bitch." JoLynn spun her around by her hair tossing her to the floor, causing Hayley to screech in pain.

"What the fuck is wrong with you? You're nuts!"

"You have no idea." She hauled her up to her feet and shoved Hayley into one of the hard wooden chairs surrounding the kitchen table. "You're so fuckin' clueless. Do you have any idea how sickening these past months have been? Huh?" She kicked at Hayley's leg, jarring the chair and she stood up, only to be shoved back down by the madwoman.

Pain radiated through her tailbone as her ass hit the wood surface. "Fuck. Really? What is your deal?"

JoLynn pinned her to the chair, pressing her shoulders to the backrest and positioned herself so she'd be eye-to-eye with Hayley. "Don't you know? Oh, of course not." She spat. "You're poor, sheltered Hayley who grew up with a horrible mother and no father. Poor, poor you." She sing-songed in a high-pitched, squeaky tone. Her eyebrows wrinkling and blue eyes like glassy daggers boring right through Hayley's own, rendering her speechless.

What a fuckin' psycho.

Even with her head throbbing, she was coherent enough to know nothing she said would please or appease the woman, so she remained silent. Hopefully, JoLynn would slip up and give her a way to call Aiden or escape.

"Now, you and I are gonna have a little chat. First of all, Aiden won't be here to save you. He's . . . otherwise engaged at the moment. Seems Tex got himself into some trouble with a few of my friends. Second, I've cut the phone lines, taken your keys off of the desk while you made that god awful coffee you gorge yourself on. Third," JoLynn swiped Hayley's cellphone off of the counter and throwing it onto the floor, shattering it into bits.

Well, fuck. Now what?

Hayley half-listened as she tried to think of a way to get out of the office.

No keys. No phone. Shit. Shit. Shit.

JoLynn pulled out a chair and scooted it until it was right in front of hers. "Now, we can have a nice little chat. Sister to sister, as it is."

What?

Hayley held her aching head between her hands, confused and still a bit disoriented, but not enough to convince her she wasn't imagining what JoLynn had just said.

"Oh, you didn't know that either?" JoLynn puckered her lips, her face twisting into an evil mask. "That sweet daddy you miss so much, the one who ruined your mama? He left yours for mine." She threw her head back, cackling and shaking his head side to side. "While you were holdin' your drunken mama's hair as she came off of bender after bender, your good ol' daddy was fuckin' mine. I'd like to say it's nice to meet ya, sis. But I've hated you my entire life." Her eyes narrowed to slits between her pinched brow and she sat there staring at Hayley with hatred . . . more than hatred, something she'd never seen before in another human being and something she couldn't explain.

"What are you talkin' about?" Hayley managed when her head began to clear.

"We. Are. Sisters." She enunciated each word slowly. "Does that help? Or do I need to draw you a picture? Well, I guess we're really half-sisters, but that's neither here nor there. We're related and I've got your vile bloodline inside of me."

Why the hatred? What have I ever done to her?

As the pounding in her head began to subside, her stomach recoiled and ached. Determined to let JoLynn believe she was still a bit foggy, she asked, "I only met you a few months ago, right? Or have we met before? Sorry, I can't think clearly with the thumpin' ya just gave me."

"Oh, don't pull the naïve and 'pity me' cards. I've known all about you since the day I was born." JoLynn got up from her chair and Hayley laid her head down on her arms on the table. "Sit up!" She spat and she grabbed a bottle of wine out of a cupboard.

Why is there wine at the office. I don't allow drinking on the premises.

"I've spent years listening to stories about you. Now," she poured some of the clear liquid into a large tumbler and pointed the half-empty bottle at Hayley. "You're gonna listen to me. Got it?"

Hayley watched as the woman chugged the entire contents of the plastic cup and then refilled it with the remaining alcohol before placing the cup on the large table. She spun on her heels and broke the glass bottle over the ceramic farmer's sink that Hayley had hand-chosen and installed herself.

Bitch! You're so gonna pay for that.

"I'd hate to mess up that pretty face of yours before it's time. Maybe I'll take a photo real quick and send it to Aiden. You know, so he can see you one last time." Jolynn removed her cell phone from the back pocket of her jeans. "Say cheese, bitch. There. Now, send. All right. Now, we can get to it."

Drink up, JoLynn. Drink it all.

"See, though he left your mama, dear ol' dad just couldn't stop talkin' about or thinkin' about you. He even made sure he let me know that I wasn't you. Constantly. *Hayley-Bird has such beautiful hair. Hayley has my eyes. Hayley would never do that. Hayley is such a smart girl. Hayley loved my truck, why can't you?* Jesus Christ, do you have any idea how little things like that fucked me up? Oh, and the kicker? He left my mama when I was around sixteen. Sound fuckin' familiar?"

She then stood, pacing while she drank from the large cup of wine. "That sonofabitch made me hate myself, treated my mama like shit and left us with nothin' and all because, get this," she laughed. "All because of you. Ha! His first born. Oh, but did he come back to you?"

Holy fuck. She was beyond batshit.

"No. He didn't. You know that, JoLynn. I already told you."

"You told me lies!" She threw the plastic tumbler at Hayley's head, missing her forehead only because she'd ducked just in time.

Covered in the smelly, stinky liquid that had gushed from the cup as it came flying at her, Hayley wiped at the alcohol that had splashed onto her head and face.

"I know he went back to you. You got it all." She smirked, walking around the kitchen with her arms spread wide. "You got his eyes, his smarts, his willingness to do whatever it takes to get what you want, his attention even though you weren't even in the same house or town for that matter. You got everything."

Oh, yeah. I got everything. Including a psychotic, drunken egg donor who beat the hell out of me. You. Ignorant. Bitch.

Hayley sat there and listened to the woman ramble on and on as the alcohol she'd imbibed did its job. JoLynn began to slur and Hayley knew she'd get one opportunity to get away before JoLynn picked up that broken glass bottle and did God only knew what to her.

"I'm so sorry." Hayley realized a second too late that the words had come out of her lips in more of a question than a sincere statement and JoLynn turned those blazing blue eyes on her in a flash.

"Oh, trust me. You will be by the time I'm done with you. You just couldn't take the hints, could ya? Even after all of the threats and I really thought that last one to Rocky would send you running and screaming for the hills to get out of this business. Or at the very least," she paused through a fit of hiccups.

Through all the extra and unnecessary 'ths' she attached to her words, Hayley remained stoic when in fact, she wanted to laugh at the sad and pathetic woman standing in front of her.

What a piece of trash.

"But, ya know," she toppled back into the seat, staring Hayley down. "I'm still gonna have it all."

"Really? How's that?"

"You're," her ability to pronounce anything quickly fading, leaving her sounding like she had a lisp. "Gonna sign this paper, bitch." From her other pocket, she fumbled and fell into a slouch before she could get the piece of folded white paper out of her skin-tight jeans. "You're gonna give it all to me. Ya know. Because ya found out we're sisters," the word sounding more like 'thithterths'. "Then, you're gonna disappear and Aiden will have no choice but to come runnin' to me. Ya never deserved him. Yeah, I know ya were together last night. Ya sucked his cock like a pro, spread your legs and let him have you when he should've been with someone like me. I tried to be like you are. Dressed in these damn ugly clothes, colored my hair that awful brown and all, but you're a whore just like your mama."

Oh, for fuck's sake. That's why she tried to make me jealous. She dressed like me, learned my business and tried to steal Aiden. All because of something our father did and out of spite. Wow.

"Maybe we should do this when you haven't had quite so much to drink." She laughed. "Because, clearly you're blitzed out of your damn mind if you even think Aiden would ever want your stupid, skanky, degenerate ass. Or that I'd sign my business over to you, for that matter. You're fucking nuts. Do you hear me? You're not the first drunk bitch I've ever dealt with. So, go eat a dick. Eat an entire bag of dicks. You're getting' nothin' from me." Hayley's laughter only agitated the delusional woman and enraged her.

"Don't fuckin' laugh at me! Sign it!" She grappled at the pens in a basket Hayley kept in the middle of the table for the drivers. When she couldn't grab one, she simply overturned the basket and flung half of the pile towards Hayley.

Even though Hayley was beyond pissed, it took all she had not to fake slur right back at her. Instead, she seized the opportunity the only way she knew how. With a swipe of her hand she threw the pens right back at JoLynn and jumped to her feet as JoLynn toppled off of the chair, her ass hitting the floor with a 'thud'. Hayley grabbed the carafe of hot coffee, opened the lid as kneeled beside the drunk woman.

"Like I said, go back to the trailer trash hole you came from. There's nothin' for ya here. Not a damn thing." When JoLynn grabbed Hayley by the hair, she dumped the hot coffee onto JoLynn's lap.

"Ouch! Oh my god! You bitch! It's meltin' my fuckin' skin off." She wailed, her screams reverberated around the massive kitchen, threatening to pierce Hayley's eardrums.

"There, now you have a real reason to take your clothes off." She stood, pinning her with a glare and with more courage than she felt, through clenched teeth she said; "Stay the fuck away from me, my dog, my business and my man. Or I will annihilate you and make you wish you'd never been born to our dear ol' dad."

"Too late for that, bitch and we're the same. Trash born from trash. What else ya got?" She whimpered while rubbing at her soaked jeans.

Hayley stooped to her level and pulled her fist back before she connected with JoLynn's cosmetically enhanced nose. "That's for fuckin' threatenin' my dog." Grabbing the tangle of hair, now blonde again, by the extensions attached to JoLynn's head, she slammed her sideways against the leg of the heavy wooden table. JoLynn slumped to the floor in a battered heap. "Dear ol' dad was right about one thing, I am smarter and better than you."

With adrenaline still pumping through her veins at breakneck speed, Hayley's thoughts returned to getting as far away from the office and JoLynn as she could. *Phone.* She snatched JoLynn's off of the table. *Keys.* Instead of searching for Aiden's, she yanked JoLynn's gaudy keychain off of the counter where JoLynn had tossed them earlier. Making her way to the door, she fumbled to get the locked deadbolt to release before she sprinted out the door. Racing around the side of the building, she located JoLynn's car hidden on the other side of a small pottery shed that Hayley used to house her gardening tools and snow shovel.

Yanking open the door of the small sports car, she threw herself inside, slamming and locking the door with her left hand as she shoved the key into the ignition. With a quick turn, the engine sputtered to life and Hayley nailed it, flying away from the office. Checking her rearview mirror, she could see JoLynn still hadn't come outside of the office building. She floored it down the gravel drive, the speedometer registering sixty-five as dust and stones trailed in her wake.

Slowing enough to make the sharp turn at the 'T' intersection, she cranked the wheel hard to the right, taking the route that would get her to the highway the quickest. The ass end of the car fishtailed in the loose stone and she quickly righted the small car and sped off, roaring across country roads with no intention of slowing down unless her heart did the same.

"Crazy fucking bitch. Holy fuck! How could I have been so stupid as to hire someone like that. My sister? What the actual fuck?"

She took deep breaths willing to calm herself enough to call the sheriff. Dialing nine-one-one, Hayley waited as it rang and rang. "Shit." The phone was losing a signal and battery life as she followed the winding country roads. "Come on. Come on. Bingo!" As she turned the corner towards the last road that would get her to the highway, she dialed Sheriff Baynes himself.

"Hayley, we're on our way."

"What?"

"Aiden and I should be there in a few. Sit tight. Are ya okay?"

"I'm not there. I left. She's a bloody mess. But I'm fine."

"What? You're breakin' up. What'd ya say?

"I beat her ass. Just go get her before she wakes up and leaves somehow!"

"Darlin', I can't understand you. Speak up."

"For fuck's sake." Hayley held the phone away from her ear to check the signal only to find it was even worse than before. She yelled, "I'm losin' ya, sheriff." Another glance at the phone, one split second more of looking away from the road. Suddenly, the car lurched to the side and she was airborne in the Italian hunk of junk and rocketing over the side of the one-lane bridge.

Pieces of rubber and red fiberglass showered over the car and in front of the windshield as the hood of the mangled vehicle tipped forward. From somewhere far away, she heard screams. They couldn't be her own. Someone was hysterical. She never got hysterical. Someone else was yelling. She, however, was falling face and hood first into the Kentucky side of the great Ohio River. Her knuckles were bone white and rigid as she gripped the steering wheel with one hand and released her seatbelt with her right so she could get out before the car would have a chance to sink, essentially trapping her in a small water-logged coffin.

Bracing herself for impact as best she could, the nose of the car hit the water first, slamming her chest into the steering wheel, knocking the wind out of her as her head bounced against the roof of the car and slammed sideways into the driver's side window with alarming force. After the initial impact and though she was dazed, Hayley absently wiped at her forehead, trails of blood leaving her fingers warm as the coppery smell filled her nostrils, sickening her. In seconds, green and icy cold liquid rushed into the car through the broken glass, engulfing her. Try as she might, her left leg wouldn't move. Feeling weightless yet, under tremendously crushing pressure, she forced herself to not open her mouth and scream.

Get out! Come on! Move! I just can't. Stuck. Can't see. Oh my god not like this! Please, please help me. Someone help me. Damn it, please!

Fear and anger screamed through her mind. She prayed and fought to stay conscious long enough to free herself. As she held her breath and continued to struggle out of whatever her foot was tangled up in, the murky depths overtook her quickly. Exhausted, she let go. Realizing that fighting the inevitable was futile, she drifted away into a dark abyss of silence and out of all the people in the world, her mother's voice rattled through her mind.

This is what you get for falling in love with a trucker. I told you it was bad luck and never ends well, didn't I?

CHAPTER NINETEEN

"Hales?" Dashing past his pickup in the driveway, Aiden crashed through the front door of the office. "Hayley! Where are ya?"

Total disarray surrounded him. The phone line lay draped across Hayley's desk, her potted plants were overturned and there was glass scattered about the hallway.

"Help me." Someone croaked, barely a whisper from somewhere in the enormous house-like building. "Please."

"Babe?" Aiden rushed into the kitchen, only to find JoLynn wadded up in the fetal position on the kitchen floor. "Where is she?"

He didn't care about the fact the woman was clearly in pain as she lay on top of shards of glass. He looked around the room and surmised the broken pieces were from the remaining wine bottle neck tucked under the kitchen table and just out of JoLynn's reach.

"She attacked me, Aiden." JoLynn sat herself upon n her elbows, pleading to him with swollen eyes, a bloody bulbous nose and a dark brown liquid dripping from her hair.

"Bullshit."

"She's crazy. All I did was stop by for my final paycheck and she flew into a jealous rage."

Aside from the dramatic emphasis she threw into her words, the woman sat there sniffling and mewling like an injured kitten. The site of it disgusted him. If JoLynn looked like this, Hayley was either perfectly fine or as badly messed up as the insane woman crawling to him across the floor. Until then, until he'd found out the truth about JoLynn, he'd never before considered hitting a woman. Now, he couldn't make any promises not to.

"Where is she?" He knew he sounded like he'd growled at her. "Tell me or I will pick up your conniving, manipulative ass by your stringy hair and shake the rest of the truth out of you. So help me, God, I will. Now!"

She flinched when he raised his voice. "I already told you. She attacked me and left. She couldn't handle the thought of us being together, Aiden. She just went nuts." Sobbing, she placed her hands on her face, crying into them.

"Us? Bein' together? Knock it the fuck off. Whatever she did to ya was deserved." Aiden squatted down, resting his forearms on his knees as he stared her in the eyes. "You're damn lucky I'm a man of integrity. But that could change. If I find out you even looked at her funny, goin' to prison will seem like winning the lottery to you. Hear me?"

JoLynn stared back at him, wide-eyed with her lips quivering. "But how can you speak to me like this? I've done nothin' to you." She wailed.

Aiden folded his hands together in an effort to refrain himself from strangling her. "You're such a narcissist. You've got no idea how much all of us already know, do ya?" He was shocked by the menacing sound of his own laughter. "You, my dear felon, are fucked. Now, where is Hayley?"

Shock and dismay lit her face as her eyes darted side to side.

"Don't even think about makin' a move. The sheriff will be here any second and he can't wait to get his hands on you. Ya fucked with the wrong people this time. There's no escape."

"Fuck you, that bitch and your stupid hick friend. Ya got nothin' on me. I'm glad the sheriff is comin'. He can take me home since your whore stole my car."

Whore?

Aiden's best bet was to get up and move away from JoLynn as quickly as he could. "Oh, you'll be takin' a ride with him all right. Sit right there. That cloud of dust out there is just what you're needin'."

JoLynn began to shake and sob again. "I'm so sorry. I didn't mean it. She got everything. Please forgive me!"

"Ya know what? Just shut-the-ever-living-fuck-up. Between what your guys did to Tex and whatever ya did to Hayley, I'm on the verge of goin' to prison for killin' ya right now. You'd better hope she's okay and if she isn't, ya better hope the sheriff has ya locked far, far away from where me or my friends I know on the inside can reach ya."

Aiden spotted his pickup keys on the floor in the corner of the kitchen, snatching them up he stomped out of the house, rushing to greet the sheriff as his Jeep slid sideways into the parking lot. "Hey . . ." the words died on his lips when the sheriff jumped out of his vehicle and ran towards him screaming.

"Something's wrong! Hayley's gone. Her phone was breakin' up, but I know she's not here. She took off, man. Somethin's not right, Aiden."

Aiden patted him on the back. "Get in there. That bitch is injured and can't get outta here on her own. I'm goin' to find her. And Baynes, lock that filthy psycho away before I put my hands on her."

"You got it."

Knowing the pickup would be easier to maneuver on the backroads and easier on fuel than the Pete would be and not knowing where Hayley might've ended up, Aiden climbed inside the heavy duty truck. He fumbled slightly with the keys before it roared to life.

I'm comin', babe. Please be okay.

As of late, it seemed he'd been down this gravel drive more than he had been in the past five years.

Hell, I've covered more miles on my off-time than I have in the big rig lately.

When he came to a stop at the end of the gravel lane, he could spot the tracks of a smaller vehicle. The gravel spray pattern was a clear sign the car had fishtailed out onto the road and headed towards Taylor's Bridge.

"Holy shit, she was drivin' that piece of shit hard." Aiden cranked the wheel to the right and followed the tire tracks.

He matted the accelerator in the hopes of catching up with her after the sheriff's words finally hit him. He'd heard Hayley screaming. There was no time to follow her trail like an old man out for a drive.

Something isn't right. JoLynn's car is already one pothole away from becomin' scrap metal and with the way she must be drivin' . . .

He dared not finish the thought and willed his truck to go faster than it already was. His heart hoped for the best, but his gut told him his girl needed him desperately. He raced on, passing secluded small forests that lined either side of the road. Out past Henderson's Farm, a deer jumped out of the brush, startling him. With a quick crank of the wheel, he avoided hitting the young buck and trucked on.

"Come on, come on. Where are ya, babe. I should've caught up to her by now. Shit." He slapped at the steering wheel. "If only I'd stopped her from leavin' this mornin'. I shoulda' put my foot down and made her stay."

The guilt tore at him and, if anything had happened to his love, Aiden didn't know what he'd do.

Stop thinkin' like that. Just find her!

When the road switched to one lane and he followed the curve around to the right, he caught sight of the ass end of the red car as it swerved side to side, shoulder to shoulder up ahead of him.

"What the hell is she doin'?" He squinted as the harsh rays of the midday sun blasted through the gaps in the trees that lined the narrow road, hitting him in the face.

The small car lurched right and before his very eyes, it changed direction and shot hard to the left, crashing over the small crumbled concrete embankment of Taylor's Bridge. Before he could scream, Hayley and the car were nosediving over the edge and headed for the Ohio River.

Reaching the scene, he slammed the truck into park and jumped out. "Hales! Oh my God, Hayley! No!"

Chunks of metal, rubber and fiberglass debris littered the road all around him as he stood powerless to stop the car from plummeting into the water.

"No no no no no no no! She can't swim." He jumped off of what remained of the bridge and dove after her, the cold water stinging his face when he broke through.

Coming up for air, he could see the trunk of the car slowly disappearing as the rushing water of the great river overtook the small vehicle in a few short moments. Wasting no time, he swam towards the spot and with a deep breath, he dove back under. He watched as the car sank deeper and deeper. The side window was clearly shattered and allowed the water to fill the small space in seconds.

Hold on, darlin'. Please hold on.

When the car finally stopped sinking, Aiden tried to get to her. Short on breath, he surged to the surface, gasping and dove back down. The car had landed on a slanted rock bed, leaving the car sitting precariously in a vertical position. With too much movement, the car could tip either way—crushing Hayley or landing right side up. Without a second thought, he began ripping at the shattered and broken glass of the driver's side window. He could see Hayley was unconscious and the injuries on her head apparent. Blood oozed out of her forehead and the water whisked it away.

Hales, don't you die on me. Damn it!

Once again, he raced to the surface, took as deep of a breath as he could and shot back down to Hayley. Reaching in through the window, he tugged at her clothing and the vehicle swayed. They were running out of time. He leaned into the car and wrapped his arms around her chest, pulling with all of his might to free her of the mangled heap. The wreckage moved slightly, but he didn't stop.

Now or never.

He tugged with all he had and her body slid free as he yanked her out of the small opening just as the car could take no more and in slow motion, it fell towards them. Aiden clung to her as he propelled them both to the surface and swam to the sandy shoreline. Later, he would remember the screaming of sirens and the yelling from somewhere above them. Right then, he was focused on one thing . . . saving the love of his life. She wasn't breathing and her heartbeat was faint. His own pulse was pounding hard enough for the both of them and if it were possible, he'd switch places with Hayley.

I'll do anything. Just don't let me lose her. I can't lose her.

He placed his hands on her chest pumping up and down, demanding she breathe with every thrust.

If it has to be someone, let it be me. Damn it, make her breathe!

He was being moved away from her body. Arms encircled his, dragging him a few feet up shore. It felt like he was being held miles away from her. In a daze, he watched as other people crowded Hayley. They were wearing uniforms of some sort and they appeared to be fussing with something. Touching her, moving her.

Save her. Stop doin' that you'll hurt her. Hey! Where are ya takin' her?

He wanted to shout, cry or whatever it took to get their attention so that he could get some answers, but he was numb.

She has to be okay. She has to be fine. Bring her back to me.

"It's okay, son. She'll be okay."

Son? I'm nobody's son. Get off me.

He shrugged off the arms that held him and darted up the side of the rocky hill. Exhausted and terrified he'd lost Hayley, his legs refused to work. Aiden slipped on the gravel and slid to the bottom, landing on his now bruised and battered knees.

"Aiden," a familiar voice, the man who'd called him 'son', called softly to him. He didn't want to look at him. If he took his eyes off of the stretcher that Hayley was on, he might miss the moment she opened her eyes. He needed her to sit up and give him a thumbs up with that goofy grin of hers.

Someone hauled him to his feet and he felt an arm go around his waist. "Come on, Aiden. We're gonna follow 'em."

Coffee! He should go somewhere and grab her a nice, big cup of her favorite coffee. She'll need that when she wakes up. She's a beast without her caffeine. Where could he go? Why are there red and blue lights everywhere? They're much too bright. Hayley needs her sunglasses. She has sensitive eyes.

"In ya go. Duck." Someone placed their hand on his head, pushing down gently. "Sit tight. You'll be with her soon."

Good. He needed to be with her. Someone should dry her clothes for her. She was so wet. So wet and tired. A nap will do her some good. He couldn't nap. Wouldn't. He needed to be there when she opened her eyes. He'd never leave her side again. Never.

CHAPTER TWENTY

One Week Later…A Few Miles Outside of Louisville, Kentucky

Warm. Whomever had brought her to this place had taken care of everything. They kept the shades pulled tightly, her bed was so soft and cozy. She never wanted to leave the safe cocoon. It was like Aiden's bed, except for a strange smell that lingered in the air. Every time she thought she'd figured out what it was . . . poof! She was back in the comfort of the fluffy bed with all thought of the odor gone in a flash.

Aiden should really get a bed like this one. Once in a while, she felt as though she were riding the ocean waves, adrift on a tiny raft under the moonlit sky. Like now, she could feel the water lapping at her toes, but they wouldn't move when she wiggled them. Strange. It was as though they were stuck.

Oh, God. My leg. Why won't my leg move? Someone help me! It's stuck!

The water isn't calm. It's coming. Coming for me. Please, please help!

"Noooooooooo!" The scream tore from her throat and she thrashed about.

"It's okay, sweetie. Calm down. You're safe."

Stop holding me down. Why are you stabbing my arm? No. No. I don't want to go back into the water. Please, no!

Aiden. Where was he? I need him. The bed is no longer warm. He keeps me warm . . . safe. The water is back. Cold, filthy water touching me everywhere. These people know I can't swim. Why do they keep sending me back into the water? What the hell? This vacation was turning out to be torture.

Maybe I should sleep. Maybe I am asleep. Am I dreaming? The water is getting deeper. Someone needs to come in here and pull the damn plug or shut it off. The moonlight is gone. I need to get home. Rocky is there. He needs me. Get me out of this water! Now. I've got to get out. This isn't funny. Someone please save me! Now, please now!

"Help me!" Gasping for air, Hayley forced her body forward.

Her throat was so raw, it felt like it was on fire. The scream that had torn from her lips wasn't as loud as it had been in her mind. It was more of a whispery echo that surrounded her. Wrapping her hands around her throat, willing it to stop aching, she finally opened her eyes. The harshly lit room blinding her at first, she couldn't stand to keep her eyelids open. Everything hurt. Each breath she took was painful. She dared not lay back down for fear the water would be there again.

The water. I'm out of the water.

"Dear God, where am I?"

She flinched when a door opened with a crash. "Good afternoon, Miss Shaw. It's good to see you're finally awake."

She squinted against the glare in the stark, white room and tried to look in the direction the voice had come from.

"Don't push yourself too hard, sweetheart. You've been through a terrible ordeal. Just lay back and relax."

"No." The forcefulness of the word wasn't intended. But she didn't care if the grandmotherly woman standing before her liked it or not. She would never lay down in that bed again.

"Hayley, I know you're scared. But, you're okay now. I promise. We've been takin' really good care of you."

She looked around, taking in more of the room around her. There were tubes and needles in her arms with machines connected to them. The smell, that same odor she'd noticed when she was sleeping lingered like a heavy cloud.

"Where am I?"

"Louisville Metro. You've been here for just over a week." The woman took Hayley's hand in her own. "I'm Mable, one of the many nurses and staff who've been waiting for you to wake up. We were beginning to think you were the real-life Sleeping Beauty." She winked and patted her hand. "Your handsome prince has been here night and day, but he just stepped out for a bit."

"I've been here that long? Why? What about my dog? Aiden was here?" Hayley erupted into fit of coughs and Mable rushed to pour her a glass of water.

"Easy now. You're going to be sore for a few days, don't try to talk very much right now. They had a tube down your throat to help you breathe. Thought we'd lost you a few times. I'm not sure why, but it seemed like you were fightin' us on comin' back." Hayley watched as she unwrapped something before handing it to her. "Here. Take a sip. The cold will help ease the pain back there."

She did as she was told and sipped the water through the clear, plastic straw Mable had placed into the pink cup. Lifting her arms to accept the cup only brought more pain. She'd felt as though she'd been hit by a MACK truck.

"What happened to me?" She whispered.

"Well, word around the hospital is that you decided to play Dukes of Hazzard in a hoopty and launched yourself off of a bridge. Let's just say you didn't quite stick the landing." Mable gave her a wink again.

In that moment, Hayley without a doubt knew that she liked the witty and sarcastic woman. Her short gray hair framed her face in a pixie cut and the wire framed glasses she wore only magnified the twinkle in her blue eyes. She wasn't plump nor thin and she moved about the room with the ease, of a woman in her twenties though Hayley would guess her to be closer to seventy. She continued to watch as Mable took her vitals and wrote a few notes on an iPad with a stylus. Her hands marked with age, showing a few liver spots but her fingers were smooth and untouched by arthritis.

"Well, looks like you'll be able to get those lines pulled out of you soon. Personally, I think they only add to your appeal. They're the latest in hospital fashion—as is that flattering sack-like hospital gown they've given you."

Hayley had to laugh at the woman's jokes. She had a personality that was infectious. Hayley's head pounded and she held it steady between her hands until a wave of dizziness subsided.

"There, there." Mable snorted. "See? That's what happens when you try to drive like the big boys. Didn't anyone ever warn you about that? Seriously, though, you suffered a concussion but that's the least of what happened. You were clinically dead once. They almost pinned you as the latest drowning statistic. Yet, here you are. It's about damn time you came around. All of us were pretty scared for ya."

The reality of what had happened slammed into her in an enormous wave of force almost knocking the wind back out of her. "Oh my god."

"Well, I'm sure He's got somethin' to do with it. However, I think He's moved onto other folks who need Him more right now." She smirked as she set about fluffing Hayley's pillows.

"Did they arrest her?"

"Who, sweetie?"

"The woman. JoLynn. I was tryin' to get away from her."

"Ah. I'm not sure about the finer details, but I reckon I did hear somethin' along those lines. In fact, I believe they brought in a woman by that very name on the very same day you arrived."

"She's here?" Panic ripped through her and she moved to yank the tubes and needles from her arms.

"Ah-ah-ah." Mable waved a finger at her. "Those stay in until the doctor says they come out. Ya hear?" When Hayley nodded, she continued. "As far as I know. She was treated and released."

"Damn it. So, the bitch is free anyways."

"Such language from such a pretty girl." She tsked.

"Sorry." Hayley felt as though she'd been scolded by her grandmother. Until that very moment, she hadn't realized how much she'd truly missed her all of these years. Mable reminded her of Grandma Gabby, short for Gabrielle and perfect for the chatty old woman, in so many ways. The way she moved, spoke and smiled were just a few. If only she were here. Mable and Gabby would make great friends.

"I was just teasin', child. No reason to get all serious on me. Wanna know a secret?" With a nod from Hayley, Mable pulled back the capped sleeve of her smock, revealing a Property of Hell's Angels tattoo on her shoulder. Mable placed a finger to her lips and winked. "We all have our naughty side, don't we?"

The woman was a character. Hayley shook her head, knowing she was grinning ear-to-ear. "I'm speechless."

"Well, good. You need to stop gabbin' anyhow. Rest and relax. I mean it. I'll be back in a few with permission to remove your gear here. But, you need to sit tight and behave. Don't go all Evel Knievel up in here while I'm gone, hear me?"

"I'll try not to." Hayley smirked and rolled her eyes, regretting the gesture immediately as needle like daggers of pain radiated through them.

Before closing the door behind her, Mable placed a palm on her hip. "If that hunky man of yours shows up before I get back, don't let him leave, okay? At my age, I need all the excitement I can get. And that man is lucky I'm not any younger. I'd ride him like I used to ride my favorite roller coaster when I was a teen—all day and all night. Mmm! Hold onto that one, lady. Or I'll be tempted to scoop him up myself."

Hayley knew her eyes must be bugging out of her head and her mouth was hanging open in pure shock.

Wow! That imagery will never go away.

She erupted into another round of coughs and laughter. The woman sure had spunk!

Mable took all of the joy out of the room with her when she left and Hayley sat there lost in her own thoughts—her own worries. She knew what had happened and she knew why. Her mother's voice hadn't stopped bickering at the back of her mind since she opened her eyes. Never in a million years did Hayley think she'd ever admit her mother had been right about anything, but she was. Now that she'd made it past her own death experience, she'd have to do the one thing that would probably kill her inside.

CHAPTER TWENTY-ONE

"Hey, darlin'." Aiden stepped into her hospital room, easing through the door with yet another large bouquet of flowers and an enormous cluster of multi-colored balloons. "Someone told me ya finally came back to us."

"Hey there, yourself."

Aiden placed the items on a counter across the room and was at her side in an instant. The need to kiss her was more than he could bear. Her beautiful eyes were swollen and puffy with a few bloodshot streaks through them and her hair was a mess. The ugly purple bruising around her face and her head injury was already healing. Tears streamed down her cheeks as she sat there, seeming so tiny and fragile wearing the unflattering hospital gown in that large hospital bed. But to Aiden, he'd never seen her look prettier.

He eased onto the bed and carefully wrapped her in his arms. "Ssh. You're okay. I'm here." He allowed her a few moments to cry into his shoulder, her tears soaking his shirt and Aiden swore he'd be her personal sponge if she needed to cry into infinity. He'd take away all of her pain, her worry and fear. She came back to him for a reason. Now, he'd never let her go.

Aiden hadn't had the easiest of weeks. After a few days of touch and go with Hayley's life at risk, he was beyond wrecked—a broken man. However, he refused to give up hope and he'd set about making sure everything Hayley needed was handled. He personally checked on Rocky throughout the day and slept at her house each night so that he wasn't alone. First thing in the morning, he returned to the hospital and sat by her bedside. Sometimes, he'd read to her and other times he'd just hold her hand and pray while silent tears streamed down his face.

Once the doctors were sure she was through the worst of it, they'd removed the breathing tube and oxygen, but they'd kept her sedated until she could wake up on her own.

"Ya surprised all of them, babe. No one thought you'd be back so soon."

She was his gift—his temperamental, hard-lovin' and beautifully imperfect gift.

"I'm so sorry, Aiden. I should've listened to you instead of leavin' you that mornin'. If I had, none of this would've happened."

"Well, yeah." He teased. "A woman should always listen to her man."

She yanked out of his arms and swatted at him with a look of shock upon her face. "Really? All ready with the jokes?"

"Well, yeah. I thought ya knew me by now." He planted a soft kiss upon her swollen lips, careful not to press too hard. "All jokin' aside, do you know how happy I am? I don't care about that mornin'. All that matters is that you're here—with me now. Got it?"

She nodded and Aiden planted kisses on her hands, bringing one to rest against his cheek. "I'd be lost without . . ." he couldn't force himself to say the words. He couldn't go back to that place in his mind where his world momentarily had shattered.

"Are you okay?"

"I am now." His vision clouded with tears, the kind he'd only hoped to cry. "Let's see how long it'll be before we can break ya outta this place, all right?"

"Can we just sit and talk for a bit first? Will you tell me what happened? I mean, the real details. I can remember most of it, but some of it is fuzzy. Must be all the drugs they've had me on."

"Sure, babe. If you're up to it. I'll do anything ya want. Where should I begin?"

"Let's go over all of it."

Aiden filled her in on Tex being attacked. "He's fine. They just released him a few days ago. He's got some stitches and he's banged up pretty bad, but Ronnie's takin' care of him."

"I can't believe that bitch did all of this harm. If I'd never hired her . . ."

"Hush. She was after you even before that."

"But, why go after all of you? Because I fired her?"

"No. JoLynn wanted to be fired and made up that whole story about goin' home so you'd think she was gone. Her guys were at the Triple F waitin' for all of us to fuel the trucks. Understand, I'd seen her talkin' to these guys before, but when I first arrived, it didn't click." He pointed to his head. "They knew we'd be there that day because JoLynn overheard you about the loads. She also knew we always do the pre-trip fuel up as a team to get the job done faster and so Mason doesn't have to do all of the trucks at his house alone."

"Such a bitch."

Aiden continued with a nod. "JoLynn paid them to tamper with the trucks. Sheriff Baynes found that out. But when Tex went inside to pay for the fuel in Mason's rig, Memphis, the fuel desk clerk, saw one of them doin' somethin' to the truck. Tex flew out there to kick some ass and he ran right into a three-on-one fight."

"I feel so bad for Tex."

"This wasn't your fault. He'll heal and the jerkoffs didn't do any damage to the trucks because Memphis spotted the idiot underneath the rig before they could. They're all goin' down for aggravated assault because they had weapons. The diversion was all part of the plan. Whether it had been to only tamper with the rigs or to deal with those guys like we did, JoLynn knew I'd be nowhere near you when she made her move."

"But, why fuck with the trucks? It makes no sense."

"Because if Mason's equipment was down and we couldn't haul the loads, you'd lose the account. JoLynn really believed she'd swoop in and take everything by defaming you all over the community. That woman's fucked in the head. Everyone knows you. They'd have never accepted her no matter what she did."

"I'm so glad that's over. Now, tell me all about Savannah and Mason."

Savannah had the baby, but I'm sworn to secrecy on details. She's still here and I'll take you to see her as soon as they say I can."

"Oh, no. What happened? And oh my god, none of you made it to get those loads. This is awful!"

"Again, hush. Mason has enjoyed playin' proud papa and this has given Savannah and him some bonding time with their new baby . . ." he'd almost slipped up.

"Baby what? Come on, tell me. Please, please, please."

"No. That's not gonna work this time. I promised. As for the loads, I called Caroline and Donna myself. As luck would have it and I'm not sure if it's good or bad luck, the next spot was rained out. Actually, it flooded. The dates were switched and now, we deadhead to Texas first. That bein' said, Tex isn't really happy about it for some reason, but I'm sure he'll tell us when he's good and ready."

"Wow. I hope everyone is okay down there."

"Yes, from what I've heard. Now, about Rocky. You're not gonna be happy about it."

Hayley's eyes grew wide and she brought her hands to her face with a look of fear. "Did that bitch do somethin' to him? Did she?"

"Whoa. Settle down. I was just gonna say that I think I'm his new favorite person. I'm sure he misses you, but I think he's called me 'dad' a few times."

"You, brat!" I swear I'm gonna kick your ass for that when I get up outta here. How dare you scare me like that?"

"Everything's fine. I've stayed with him every night and checked on him many times each day. He's gonna be real happy to see ya. In fact, you'll be proud of him. He hasn't once made a mess on those potty squares you lay down. And yeah, we're tight." He held up his hand, crossing his fingers. "Like this."

After their giggles subsided, Hayley looked him in the eye. "What about JoLynn. God, even sayin' her name makes me want to vomit."

"Well, what exactly happened between the two of ya? That place was a wreck when I arrived. She was bleedin' and covered in somethin'. Glass was everywhere, plants were scattered all over your office. Did you have a WWE match in there or what?"

Hayley explained everything and he pressed a hand to his mouth to keep from laughing at the fact that his little spitfire had gone kamikaze. "You kicked her ass. I mean, seriously. She could barely move when I got there."

"Fucking good. She deserved worse, but I had to get outta there. Had to."

"Well, Baynes had his officers bring her here to get patched up and she's been sittin' in a jail cell ever since. After she's faced with charges here, she'll be shipped back to the hell pit she came from to face some others. She won't be gettin' outta prison anytime soon. Believe me. Not for what she's done. I'll make sure of it."

"Thank God."

"Your office has been cleaned up and all traces of her ever being there are gone."

Hayley touched the stitches on her forehead. "Well, almost all traces."

"It'll be okay, babe. I'll be here. I'm never leavin' your side again. I promise you." And he never broke a promise.

She pulled her hands away from his. "About that. Aiden, I love you, but I don't think I can do this."

Blindsided, Aiden shook his head. He must've heard her wrong. "What? Do what?"

She lowered her eyes, refusing to look at him. "This. Us." She whispered.

"What do ya mean?" He stood though his knees were weak. "Ya can't possibly mean that. Not after everything that's happened."

"I don't want it to be true, but I know this was a sign. Bein' with you, makin' love with you and lovin' you caused all of this. I tried to fight it all of this time. I swore I wouldn't love you, but the truth is I always have. Acting on that love led us to where we are right now. I almost died Aiden. What if it had been you? What if you had died? I couldn't go on. And I can't sit at home worrying twenty-four-seven about you out on the road anymore. Especially not now. I'm not made for this. I'm not made for this life."

"It's the meds talkin'. This can't be real. Are ya kiddin' me?"

"Mama always said that it was bad luck to love a trucker. I'm bad luck. This all happened because of me."

"Fuck her, Hayley. Fuck that woman and fuck the shit you're sayin'. When are ya gonna stop listenin' to the bullshit she filled your head with? What? Are ya just gonna live alone all your life? Or find some doctor or lawyer to marry? That's not you and ya know it."

She flinched at his harsh tone and he didn't give a damn. Pacing the room in silence, he forced himself to calm down. "Look," he returned to her bedside. "I'll give it all up. I'll find another job. I can do anything."

Crying, she shook her head. "No, Aiden. I can't ask you to do that."

"Then don't. Just nod. Just snap your fingers. Blink. I'll do whatever it takes. I don't want to lose you, Hales. Why don't you ever listen to the advice your daddy gave you instead? Why can't you just fly, Hayley-Bird? Take a real damn chance for once in your life."

"I did. Now look at me." When he shook his head. "Aiden, don't."

"Don't what? Love you? Too damn late, darlin'. Too damn late. I know you've just been to Hell and back, but damn it. This is not how it ends. This is not how we end. We don't end."

"I'm sorry." He watched as she swiped at her tears with her fingertips.

"Don't be sorry. Listen to me. I'm promisin' to do whatever you need me to do. I want to spend my life with you." *It's pointless. You should've known better, too. You're born to lose over and over again.* "If you won't let me do that, if you won't let me build a life with you as a trucker, just say the word. I can give it all up. The road doesn't own me. I'm not married to it. I should be married to you. If you can't handle that, I'll grab that goodbye gear and fly. But you'll regret it. In your heart, ya know ya will."

He waited and waited for her to say she'd changed her mind. The ticking of the wall clock hanging on the opposite side of the room drove him insane as the seconds ticked by without a word from either of them until he broke the silence.

"All right, then." He walked toward the door and stopped. Looking up at the ceiling when she still refused to meet his eyes. "I'll always love you, darlin'. That'll never change. Come find me when ya choose to live instead of just existing in that box you've built around yourself."

CHAPTER TWENTY-TWO

One Month Later

"Come on, little guy. We're ready to go."

Rocky bounced and pranced at her feet as she loaded the last of the cardboard boxes into the moving trailer she'd rented and shut the door, locking it up tight. It'd been a month since she'd last seen Aiden, but she hadn't stopped thinking about him or what he'd said. He was right. She needed to live. It was time. Locking the door to the office building one last time, she placed the keys in the loose floorboard of the deck—a predetermined place she and the realtor had decided upon when Hayley had signed the sales agreement.

With a deep sigh, she walked away feeling lighter and happier than she had in years. "All set." Holding the truck door open, Rocky hopped up into the cab and she slid in after him. "Just a few more stops and then . . . well, let's just see what happens."

Letting go of the work she'd spent so many years on hadn't been an easy decision, but it had been necessary. She'd carried the burden of so many other people for so long that she hadn't looked at all of her own wants and needs in life. Spending a few weeks in the Smoky Mountains with her faithful companion had helped. Relaxing, thinking and renewing her spirit was what she'd needed. Time away was what had truly healed her of everything that had been holding her back.

She'd never forget what happened with JoLynn and it saddened her to think that her mere existence had done so much harm to an already stunted soul. Hayley hadn't spoken to her father in years and for once, she was grateful for that. Tearing into him for creating such a monstrous child and truly crazed woman would give her only immediate pleasure. In the long run, it wouldn't change a thing. Hayley had to be the changing factor for her own sanity.

Heading away from her old life, she followed the road that she'd nearly died on. Well, she had died but somehow made it through. "This is the first time I've been back here and the last time I'll ever go this way. But I've got to face it so I can move forward."

When she reached Taylor's bridge, or what was left of it, she eased the truck onto the shoulder. Leaving the air conditioning on for Rocky, she climbed out and took deep breaths as she inched her way closer to the embankment. In the time she'd spent away from Aiden, she'd learned he'd been the one to save her. He jumped from the very spot she was standing and dove in after her. If he hadn't gotten there in time, there'd have been no coming back—no second or third chance. He was a man of integrity and he loved her more than his own life. Instead of embracing his love, she'd tossed him away. Instead of kissing him in that hospital room, she'd broken his heart.

Sheriff Baynes filled her in on everything he'd said while trying to resuscitate her until the paramedics had taken over.

Aiden had lost it. *"He had a complete mental breakdown, Hayley. He truly believed you were gone."* The sheriff told her everything without a hint of judgement in his voice. He'd sat right on her front porch with her sipping sweet tea on the day she'd left for the mountains. *"There aren't many men like him. Just give it some thought, okay?"*

She promised she would. Just like she'd promised the man who'd lied and had another family behind her and her mother's backs. She made promises daily to drivers and clients. Yet, in all of Hayley's years, only one person had ever made and kept any promises to her. As hard as she tried to convince herself, she knew she'd never stop loving Aiden. But was love ever enough? She could only hope.

Hayley tossed a handful of rocks over the side of the short, crumbled wall and released her fears as the pebbles tumbled and scattered into the water below. Dusting her hands off as she made her way back to the truck, a sense of peace filled her once more. She was finally doing things that made her happy—made her feel alive. After what she'd been through, she wanted to feel that way every moment of every single day until her maker called her home—or however that worked.

"On the road again," she sang as they made their way through the hillsides and bumpy roads that only a pickup could handle.

Fifteen minutes later, she was pulling into the long driveway and parking lot that surrounded Mason and Savannah's property. She could see Savannah standing on the front porch waving. Even from a distance, Hayley could see the infinite smile on her friend's face that only being a mother could bring to a woman. Mason waved from the large pole barn and began the long trek across the gravel toward her truck.

Clipping a leash to Rocky's collar, she held him until they were both out of the truck. Normally, she didn't need to keep him tethered, but with the amount of property the Kaine's owned and after not being around them for a while, she thought it best.

"Can't have you runnin' off, can we?" He looked at her, tilted his head with a snort as if to say, "Do you even know me?" She reached into the backseat of the extended cab and carefully grabbed a large gift bag.

"Hey there, stranger." Mason wrapped his arms around her, lifting her off the ground in a giant bear hug. "How are ya?"

"Good. Really good." But, can ya put me down now?"

"Oh, sorry. I'm just so glad to see you alive and in one piece." He chuckled. "I've been worried about ya."

"I know and I'm sorry about that. Everything's fine. I've brought everything from the office that Ronnie will need. I'm sure you've filled her in on how all of this works."

Mason toed at the dusty gravel. "Yeah, she's a quick study. Caroline has her all set up for our Texas run and she's been very patient with Ronnie." he adjusted the ball cap on his head and looked her in the eye. "You're sure this is what ya want?"

"I've never been more sure. I've enjoyed workin' with all of you, but it was just time to do something else. I saved and saved for years. I figure I should at least spend some of it. Can't take it with me, ya know?" She shrugged with a smirk. "Now, can I finally meet this baby of yours?"

"You bet." He held out his hand in an offer to carry the enormous gift bag.

"How 'bout you handle Rocky so I can have both hands ready to hold this baby?"

"Deal."

Mason took control of the leash and followed Rocky's lead while Hayley headed up the steps to greet Savannah with open arms.

"You look amazing! Motherhood look good on you." She held her friend's hands, eyeing her up and down.

"Ya say that now, but you should've seen me in that hospital. I don't think those nurses and doctors have ever heard a lady cuss so much. And I doubt they'd ever heard so many . . . shall we say colorful come out of a woman in labor." Savannah laughed and her long blonde waves blew about her face in the light breeze coming from the west.

"Oh, I'm sure. I'd be the same way if it were me and . . .," She stopped herself and choked back her emotions.

"Aww, sweetie. It'll all work out. Hopefully, someday, you won't have to have a C-section like I did though. I wouldn't wish that on anyone. Girl, it's been rough."

"I didn't know. Sorry you had to go through that. Why the sudden change from natural to goin' that route."

"Stubborn child did a flip and refused to come out. Decided to be breech and there was no room or time for turning once my umbilical cord became wrapped around the baby's neck." Though Savannah had joked for a second, her eyes became glassy and her voice cracked. "It was a very close call. But my angel is fine now and perfectly healthy."

Hayley hugged her friend again. "Is that why they kept you at the hospital so long?"

"I was hemorrhaging afterward and the baby needed some extra TLC. Instead of risking the health of both of us, they kept us a few extra days until they knew we were both out of the woods. I'm so sorry we didn't make it down to see you."

"Oh, please. You had enough on your plate. I'm the sorry one. I was supposed to be there for you. The fact that you and Mason sent flowers while you were in the midst of what you were goin' through was truly amazing. Thank you."

Savannah waved her hand as if to say, "It was nothing."

"Ya know, I've really missed Mason and you, but can I please meet this baby now? The suspense is killin' me and I'd say holdin' the newest family member is long overdue."

"Absolutely. Let's go."

Savannah led the way into the expansive home and Hayley placed the gift bag on their dining room table as they made their way through the first floor and into the room Mason had turned into the nursery. Hayley had heard all about the way he'd handpicked everything, with input from Savannah, of course. They'd painted the walls in a shade they'd quibbled about for days. The baby furniture was white and not what Hayley had expected, but she had to admit that it tied the entire room together.

"I honestly expected him to create a crib out of an old Pete."

"Don't think it didn't come up in conversation." Savannah raised an eyebrow at Hayley. "Here we go. Hayley, meet Dallas Wyatt Kaine."

"Ohhhh, he's so . . . ohhh." She tried to wave the tears away before Savannah gently placed him in her arms. "Savannah, he's perfect. But where did you come up with that name?" Turning her attention to the darling boy in her arms, she snuggled him close, inhaling that uniquely baby scent that made women's ovaries melt.

"He truly is. I get all choked up every time I look at him. I can't believe how blessed we are. He's a miracle. As for his name, Mason loves the Cowboys and the only family I could ever really count on was my late grandfather, Wyatt Somers. There you have it."

"He truly is a miracle and I think his name is perfect. Look at those tiny fingers. He looks like both of you. Mason's dark hair and your golden eyes. He's a little heartbreaker all ready. Oh, I just want to cuddle with him forever. Hello, little one. I'm your aunt Hales and I'm gonna spoil you rotten. Yes, I am." She planted a light kiss on his tiny hand which held her thumb tightly. "You've got quite a grip there, Dallas." Turning to her friend, she said; "Thank you."

"For what?" Her smile, warm and sisterly.

"For allowing me to be a part of your lives. This means the world to me. I wasn't sure how things would be after what happened between Aiden and me."

"Oh, sweetheart. All of that will work out and do you honestly think we'd change our minds about ya because of something personal between you and Aiden? We're all friends—family even. That will never change. Hear me?"

Hayley nodded, grateful to have met such amazing people who had accepted her as one of their own. As she looked down at baby Dallas, she couldn't help but acknowledge the ache deep inside her heart, the hole that'd been left when she'd destroyed the relationship between her and Aiden.

This could've been my life someday.

CHAPTER TWENTY-THREE

It had been one month. One very long month. He'd spent every waking hour trying not to think of her, worrying about her, still loving her and he'd failed miserably. He missed Hayley—needed her. Without her in his life, even as a friend, he felt incomplete and part of him was pissed off about it. Aiden wondered what he'd say when he did see her again. How would he be able to look her in the eyes knowing she was leaving town?

Pulling into Mason's drive, he realized he was about to find out. "Sonofabitch."

Mason waved to him from under one of the giant oaks that lined the front of the property. Aiden spotted Hayley's truck and then, Rocky at Mason's feet. It appeared he and Rocky were having a good ol' time.

She's here.

He felt like he'd been sucker punched.

"Hey, man." He nodded as he climbed from the truck and made his way over to where Mason stood. "Set me up, huh?"

He raised his hands in mock surrender as Rocky pawed at his legs, begging for Aiden's attention. "Don't blame me. I'm not the matchmaker around here. Although, I agree it's time the two of you got over yourselves. You've been sulkin' long enough. If I have to be out on the road with you for a month, ya need to let things go and get over it or get it together. If that means sayin' goodbye before she leaves," he hitched his thumb towards the large house, "so be it. But, you will have a proper goodbye. No stormin' off. No fightin'. There's a baby here and he don't need no yellin'. Got it?"

Aiden rolled his eyes.

Total fuckin' set up.

"Man, it's over. We all know it. Why couldn't ya just let things be? I don't need this shit. Do ya honestly think I want to see her right now? I put it all on the line and she flat out made it clear she didn't want me. I'm not goin' through this again. I'll stop back some other time. Give Savannah and Dallas my love."

Reaching down, he patted Rocky on the head. "Bye, little dude. Take good care of your mama for me. Later, man." His meaningful stride away from the house was abandoned with one word coming from behind him.

"Aiden?"

Damn it all to hell. Shit.

He bowed his head slightly and pinched the bridge of his nose between his forefinger and thumb for a moment before turning around. Coming face to face with the only woman he'd ever love.

"Hayley." He didn't know what else to say.

"It's good to see ya."

Really? That's why I haven't heard from you in a month.

He slid his hands into the front pockets of his jeans and tried to look anywhere but directly at her again. He couldn't.

"I'll just leave you two alone. Remember what I said. Play nice." He nodded his head at them and led Rocky away.

The silence between them, even in the open air on the Kentucky hillside, was so thick it made his chest ache. The sunlight danced on the light colored strands of hair that were now weaved through her usual hair color and he had to admit he preferred the way her hair used to be. With every surly thought that ran through his head, he knew he was being a stubborn ass, but he wouldn't let her see how badly her words had hurt him weeks ago. No, it had been more than that—she'd destroyed him in a blaze of bullshit excuses and he was left with the ashes of what might've been. Nothing more.

Still, he couldn't just stand there saying nothing. "Heard ya were leavin'."

"That's the plan." He watched as she took a deep breath. "I've had a lot of time to think."

"I suppose so."

Another long silence fell between them, growing more uncomfortable by the second. How could he feel like shaking some sense into her and walking away at the same time? Standing there, the pain was still too fresh, his heart was too raw. Small talk just wasn't something he could do right then.

"Okay, then. Well, wherever ya go, be safe. I've gotta get goin'. We roll out next week and I've got shit to do. Goodbye, Hayley."

As his hand reached out to open the door of his pickup, she stopped him in his tracks. "I'm so very sorry Aiden."

He didn't want to hear it. Not again and in that moment, he could take no more. He marched over to where she stood, gently grabbed her arms and looked her in the eyes. "Sorry for what, Hales? What exactly are you sorry about? Leavin'? Don't let me stop ya."

"I'm . . . I'm sorry I hurt you. I'm sorry that I allowed my stupid mother to get inside my head again. I'm sorry that I threw your heart away like it didn't matter. And I'm sorry that I practically shoved you out of my life as if you were nothing to me. I'm sorry for sayin' I couldn't be with you when that's all I want—need. I'm sorry for all of it. Every damn word, every damn day that we've been apart because of me and my big fuckin' insecurities, I've missed you, loved you."

Aiden's hands dropped to his sides and he shook his head. "So, what?" He noticed his laughter had a slightly maniacal tone to it. "You went to the mountains and had some huge epiphany about life or some shit and now, you're sorry? I'm sure you'll understand if I call bullshit on this one."

"But, I . . .,"

"Don't. Just don't, Hales. We went over this in the hospital. I can't do it again."

"Please, don't go." She begged. "I know I was wrong. I knew I was wrong before the words came out of my mouth in that hospital. I was scared. Scared of lovin' you, scared of losin' you. I thought if I shoved you away, I wouldn't have to feel any of that anymore. But I was so very wrong. I felt more. I felt worse. What I did to you is unforgivable and," she sniffled. "I know I ruined everything. I just wanted you to know it was all me. It wasn't you."

"Oh, I know it was you. I was there. Remember? What I can't figure out is why? Why, Hayley? How could you think what you did was good for either of us? Why make up shit about how you're not strong enough and how you wouldn't be able to handle it? Why bullshit me? I know you. You're stronger than anything life can throw at you and yet, lovin' me, bein' with me is what made you flip out? After all of these years we finally had our moment and you pissed all over it. Why would you do that?"

"Because I'm an idiot, okay? Because I didn't think I deserved a man like you—one who'd jump into a ragin' river to save my stupid life. Because lovin' you would mean I'd have to let go of all that shit that's held me down. I wasn't ready to do that. Do you know what it's like to have somethin' else controlling your every move, every thought?"

"Of course I do."

"I had to find a way to let that go."

Aiden inhaled deeply. Here she was pouring her heart out to him and all he wanted to do was take her into his arms, quiet her with his mouth and forget all that had happened. But what kind of man would he be if he took her back after she'd broken him. What if she changed her mind again? Then what?

"Aiden, I love you. I haven't exactly been the woman you've needed, but I'm here now. I'm here for you. For us. If there's even an us to hold onto. If not, I'll go. I won't hold it against you. You told me I'd regret what I said in the hospital and I do. More than you could ever possibly know. But if you . . ."

Fuck pride.

Aiden scooped her into his arms and did what he'd been wanting to do for weeks. His lips claimed hers, kissing her as if his life depended on it. Maybe it did. He hadn't felt this alive since their night together and not since the day the doctors told him Hayley would live—that she'd be okay.

Walking her backwards, he pressed her back against one of the large oak trees and lifted her legs around his waist. He placed his hands on her cheeks and stared into her eyes. "Hales, no more talk. No more wasted time. I might be a man, but I'm not a stupid one. My pride kept me from chasin' ya down to those mountains in Tennessee, but I won't allow it to keep me away from your lovin' arms another minute. You've always had my heart. We have some mendin' to do, but time will take care of that."

"Really? You forgive me?"

"As far as I'm concerned, there's nothing to forgive. That wasn't you speakin' back in that hospital bed. It was fear and I've never backed down from fear. I'm not sure why I allowed myself to buckle that day, but I regret it just as much as you do—if not more."

She planted what felt like a hundred kisses all over his face and her smile lit up the flame that had been slowing dying inside of him. "Are ya sure about this?"

"That depends."

"On?"

"Where are ya headed?"

She looked at him sheepishly. "Wherever you're headed. I'm already packed. The house and office are on the market."

"Wait. Did you come here expectin' things to go this way?"

"No." With a shake of her head, she continued, "but I was prayin' they would. I was hopin' you'd give me another chance."

Tilting his head to the side, "Even if I wanted to, I couldn't deny you. So, ya wanna go to Texas? I hear everything's bigger there."

"I thought you'd never ask. But, for the record, I don't need bigger. I just need you."

"Well, I should probably warn ya. Things go wrong out on the road. Tires go flat, wiring needs fixed. You're not gonna flake on me again and blame yourself or us for being together, are ya?"

Her eyes blazed and she huffed.

"Too soon, darlin'?" He chuckled.

"Much, much too soon. But I've missed hearin' ya call me that."

"Well, I guess I'll just have to find other ways to tease ya."

"I can think of a few and I've heard they're illegal in Texas."

Their long, leisurely kiss was hot enough to burn the bark right off the tree as their bodies melded to each other. Without skipping a beat their hearts were back to pulsing the same steady staccato. Like a phoenix, their love rose from the ashes of what had been so wrong in their lives for so many years, placing them back on the path fate had planned for them since the very beginning.

EPILOGUE

"C'mon, you two. Knock it off all ready. All this gropin' and grab-ass goin' on. This place is like a damn brothel."

"Mason, hush. They're in love. Let them say goodbye." With baby Dallas in her arms, she leaned against her husband and planted a tender kiss on his cheek.

"Geesh. The two of you are just as bad." Aiden rolled his eyes before planting one on Hayley.

"Okay, so we all need to get a room. Mason and Savannah have plenty." Hayley laughed.

"I wish y'all could stay. But ya need to get movin'."

"I don't know if I'm all healed up yet, Mason. I need some more of Ronnie's, ahem, help." Tex said with a wink as he grabbed Ronnie's ass.

"Shut the hell up and get in that rig. These rides won't pull themselves." Turning to his wife and baby boy, Aiden could see he wasn't as ready as he claimed to be. Fatherhood had changed him and in a good way.

"I'll see the two of you soon." First he held his son and then he pulled his wife into his free arm and kissed her like it'd be the last time he'd ever see her.

Savannah's eyes were glassy after their long embrace and Aiden felt for her. Each of them; Mason, Tex and himself all had women now. With Mason having a family, Aiden couldn't stop thinking about having one of his own with Hayley. Whether they had a baby or not, didn't matter. As long as they were together, he'd always have a home and he'd make sure she always felt safe.

Ronnie and Tex were the ones who acted like horny rabbits. They couldn't keep their hands off of each other.

"I'll miss you, babe." Ronnie wrapped her arms around Tex's neck and he swung her in a wide circle.

"You better. We'll make up for lost time when I get back. Plus, we can talk on the phone each night before bed."

"Dirty talk?" She wiggled her eyebrows and flashed him that devilish grin that all of them had seen way too many times lately.

If they didn't separate them soon, none of them would ever get on the road. "Can we go now? These two are about two seconds from another round of mattress rodeo." Aiden shook his head, but deep down, he loved the fact that they'd all found happiness and love.

"Damn, man. You're as bad as Mason. Gonna start callin' you Dad number-two."

Hayley rushed up the porch steps for one final hug from Savannah and to fuss over Dallas. "I'll see y'all soon. You be good for your mama and I'll bring ya back a big ol' Texas-size present." Reaching for her friend again. "If ya need anything, call. Don't try to be so strong. Cry when ya need to and know that I'll watch over all of them as best as I can. I'll keep Ronnie and you posted when we're on the road and when they're too busy to talk. Okay? And I'll let y'all know how it goes with Romeo once we meet up. I promise."

"Hayley, I'm gonna miss all of y'all somethin' fierce. Be safe and try to keep those guys outta trouble."

"I'll do my best. Ronnie, if ya need help figurin' any of the codes or paperwork out, give me a holler. I'll help as much as I can. Again, thank you for takin' on this heavy load. It ain't easy by any means, but I know you're perfect for it. You tamed the wild Tex over there, so this won't be a problem at all."

"Don't worry, Hales. It's all under control. You just relax and enjoy your new journey."

"Damn, I'm gonna miss you ladies and my tiny gentleman. Group hug."

"Are ya sure Rocky can't stay here with us? We'll spoil him for ya?" Savannah asked with a twinkle in her eye.

"Nah. He loves to ride. We'll just tuck him in his crate when we need a bit of alone time. He'll be fine. Damn, I'm gonna miss you ladies and my tiny gentleman. Group hug." Hayley opened her arms wide, embracing the two women who'd become as close as sisters to her—the way sisters were supposed to be.

The other two ladies squeezed her tight and Aiden watched with admiration as he saw Hayley becoming more and more a part of his world and his friends' lives—his life. He never dreamed in a million years he'd call himself lucky in anything other than gambling. Especially, when love hadn't been something he'd ever wanted to risk. Hayley was different and she was taking just as much of a leap of faith as he was. They'd learn together and hopefully, someday, they'd be as blessed as Savannah and Mason were.

"Okay. Chop-chop." Mason whistled. "Load 'em up!"

"Roll on, boys!" Savannah shouted as they all climbed into their rigs.

Aiden watched as Savannah flickered the porch light on and off as they pulled out of the drive one after the other. Once they were all on the road, she left the light on. Something he'd only learned about since being around Mason and his wife. That was her way of wishing them a safe journey and the light would stay on until they were all back home where they belonged.

"She's somethin' else, isn't she?"

"She sure is." He looked at Hayley tucked safely into the passenger seat of the Pete. "Because of her, we're all together."

"I wouldn't have it any other way."

"Good thing, darlin'. 'Cause you're stuck with me for the long haul. Sweetheart, do ya think we'll ever be as lucky as Sav and Mason are?"

"Aiden, I'd say we already are. We've both been through hell and back. We're here together now. What more could we need or want?"

"Nothin' that I know of. I love everything about you and that even includes your weird packing rituals." He teased.

"Hey! Things go in a certain place. It just makes sense to do it my way. You'll see that someday." She pointed a slender finger at him.

"Yeah, I suppose I will. Does that mean someday you'll be my wife?"

"I don't know."

He whipped his head to the right so fast, he thought he gave himself whiplash.

Hayley erupted into a fit of laughter. "Joking. I was just kidding. You should've seen your face." She pointed at him and was truly enjoying the stunt she'd pulled.

"Ha, funny girl."

"You know ya love me."

"Yes. Yes I do, darlin'." He took her hand in his, kissing the soft skin of her palm.

When they rolled up to the fueling plaza at Triple F for their pre-trip fuel up, she unbuckled her seat belt and plopped onto his lap.

"Nothin' would make me happier than spendin' the rest of my life with you, Aiden Hunt. Whether we get married or not. I'll be by your side."

She kissed him long and slow until Tex and Mason began pounding on his door.

"What the hell, Phoenix? Are ya gonna fuel up or fiddly-fuck around all night?" Tex questioned.

"Well, Hales just agreed to be my wife, sort of. So maybe I will. After all, we should celebrate this right." Hayley took his hand and led him to the bunk in the back.

"Congratulations. You coulda picked a better time to ask her, Aiden. Like before now."

"Wooohoooooo!" Tex cheered. "About damn time, you two got it together!"

Before closing the privacy curtain, Aiden heard Mason yell. "Oh, for fuck's sake. Ya couldn't wait 'til later? What am I supposed to do with all of ya? Oughta start callin' ourselves the Asphalt Hornballs. Shit. Selfish bastards. I could be doin' that too, ya know. Damn it. Make it quick. We gotta roll. Sonofabitch."

Aiden heard nothing else except the fast and steady racing of their hearts as they christened his Pete and sealed the deal. He didn't care if anyone heard them or noticed the truck rocking. Having the woman of his dreams—the woman who was his heart and home, by his side was all that mattered. Aiden had fought his entire life to be back on top and with Hayley, he was on top of the world. Every lonely night, every endlessly long moment without her was forgotten. There was only the future and wherever their path took them.

"I love you, Hayley-Bird."

"I love you more, Phoenix."

"Better get dressed. It's time to get this bob-tailin' hammer lane gang on the road before Mason blows a gasket. South bound and down."

"I'm ready. With you, I'm ready for anything."

ALSO IN THE ASPHALT COWBOYS SERIES:

RENEGADE

COMING SOON:

TEX

ROMEO

OTHER BOOKS BY MADISON

RIVER JEWEL RESORT SERIES

ANYTHING YOU WANT

HUNTER'S FORTUNE

LONG OVERDUE

CLAIMING SCARLET

SMOKY MOUNTAIN ESCAPES

NATURAL LUST

YOU'LL NEVER BE LONELY

PARANORMAL/ROMANCE/HUMOR

WICKED BY NATURE

EROTICA NOVELLAS

ONE NIGHT WITH A SWAMP SHIFTER

SUBMITTING TO THE SHIFTERS

HUNTING THE HEADLESS HORSEMAN

THE LIBRARIAN

ABOUT THE AUTHOR

"Madison Sevier brings a fresh and exciting voice to the world of fiction."—CSR Reviews

The Coffee Queen of Romance spends her days pressing coffee beans into a magical potion that allows her to bring life to unique and lovable characters in realistic worlds you'll want to fall into. Against a romantic backdrop of the Ohio River and surrounding hillsides, she creates contemporary and paranormal romance stories that work their way into the hearts of readers worldwide.

Actually, she just drinks a lot of coffee and hopes for the best.

Some of her favorite hobbies include; extreme coffee research (drinking), mug collecting, hiking, writing, reading, baking and horseback riding.

She loves hearing from her readers and meeting new ones, so feel free to contact her anytime. If you sign up for her newsletter, Sevier-ly Addicted to Romance, you'll stay up to date with all things Madison and you'll also be entered into a monthly drawing.

Subscribe here: http://madisonsevier.com/
Email: madisonsevier9@gmail.com
Twitter: @MadisonSevier
Instagram: @madison_sevier
Facebook: Madison Sevier, Author

Made in the USA
Lexington, KY
03 May 2017